Exotic

Vc

By M.S. Parker

Copyright © 2015 Belmonte Publishing LLC
Published by Belmonte Publishing LLC.
ISBN-13: 978-1512041354

ISBN-10: 1512041351

Table of Contents

Chapter 1

Reed

I'd spent the last two weeks trying to convince myself that this was what I wanted to do, where I wanted to be. I'd spent three more days in Venice, but that was mostly because I'd forgotten my luggage on the train when I'd run off with...*her*.

I could've bought new clothes, but I'd decided against it in favor of spending the time drinking while I'd waited for them to be shipped back. The next day, I'd bought a new ticket to Madrid and left, hoping the memories would stay in Venice.

They hadn't.

I'd partied in Spain, drinking enough that I'd spent most mornings hanging over the toilet. After a week, I'd moved on to Lisbon, Portugal. Two days ago, I'd given up on the cities and headed to my family's villa in France. It was just outside of Marseille, perfectly located for a trip in to the city, to enjoy what it had to offer, but far enough away that I could have quiet if I wanted it.

I'd tried quiet yesterday. It had ended with me

drinking pretty much everything in the villa and passing out on the floor until past noon today. Tonight, I planned to head into the city and see if I could find someone to take my mind off things. I'd been focusing on alcohol rather than sex, but I think that might have been why I couldn't stop thinking about her.

I ran my hand down my face.

Her. Nami Carr. Fucking Princess Nami. Meeting her had been chance, but everything that had followed had been choice. Hers and mine. I'd intended for it to be nothing more than a fling. A fun one, but a fling nonetheless. I'd had dozens of them during my trip, and none of them stood out. I could barely tell one from the other in my memory. Blondes and brunettes – no red-heads because I hadn't wanted to be reminded of Piper – they all blurred together. Some had been aggressive, liking it rough. Others had wanted me to be gentle. I remembered bits and pieces of what we'd done. The positions we'd fucked in, a little kink here and there.

Except for Nami. I could remember every detail of my time with her. How her body had felt beneath mine. The sounds she'd made...

I bolted off the couch and headed for the bathroom. There was no doubt about it. I needed to get laid. The lack of sex had to be the reason I couldn't stop thinking about her. I needed someone else to get my mind off of the pretty princess.

I splashed some cold water on my face, ran my hands through my hair and then headed into my bedroom to find what I wanted to wear. The villa wasn't as large as my family's home in Philadelphia, but it was big enough to have a bedroom for my parents, myself, my younger sister Rebecca, and a guest room, as well as two bathrooms, a full kitchen, dining room and living room. My parents had bought it for family vacations. I hadn't been here in years though. Running the Stirling family business hadn't left much time for vacations. Hell, I'd even cut my honeymoon short.

I snorted a laugh. Honeymoon. The entire marriage had been a joke. I hadn't wanted to marry Britni Michaels and she hadn't wanted to marry me either. Sure, we'd slept together, but there'd been no passion, no real attraction. We'd done what we'd needed to do. I'd never asked who she'd been thinking of when we'd fucked, but I sure as hell hadn't been thinking about her. I waited for the familiar burst of shame and guilt but didn't feel it. For the first time since I'd left Philadelphia, I could think of the entire mess without any strong emotion. I was pretty sure that Piper had been right when she'd told me that what she and I'd had hadn't been real, and this was further confirmation of it. That was a relief. I wasn't in a hurry to rush home, but at least now I knew that when I did, I'd be able to handle it.

I gave myself a glance in the mirror, thought about trying to smooth down the mess of gold that was my hair, then decided against it. I knew I looked tired, but I also knew it wouldn't matter. I was a good-looking guy. I wouldn't have trouble getting a woman to come back with me. I looked away from the mirror before I could see the doubt in the near-black pools of my eyes. Not doubt about my ability to get a woman. Doubt about whether or not I really wanted to.

I pushed the thought aside and headed out to the garage. We had three cars here and our groundskeeper kept them all in excellent shape. I chose my favorite – the black Spyder – and drove in to Marseille to see what I could find.

A couple hours later, I had a bit of a buzz, but not so much that driving was a bad idea. I also had a tall, thin blonde wearing a dress that probably should've been classified as a handkerchief. Said handkerchief was currently riding up so that I could see the tiny string of red lace that made up her thong as well as her firm ass. I could see this because she was on her knees in the passenger's seat despite my strong objections that this was dangerous. Her breasts were pressed against my arm, her hand rubbing my half-hard cock through my pants. This was my compromise. She'd originally been trying to get her hand down my pants while promising to do things with her mouth that I was pretty sure were illegal in most places in the States.

When we got to the villa, she climbed out of the car, gave me a grin and pulled her dress over her head, dropping it onto the floor of the garage. She wasn't wearing a bra and her rose-colored nipples jutted out from her small breasts. Her thong barely covered more in the front than it did in the back, the sheer fabric leaving absolutely nothing to the imagination.

"Is this your car as well?" she asked as she turned to the car to our right. Her words were heavily accented, but understandable.

"My family owns all three cars," I said, looking across the top of the Spyder at her.

She cast a grin over her shoulder as she walked over to the Aston Martin and bent over the hood, giving me an even better view of her ass.

"What are you doing?" The question was stupid. It was obvious what she was doing.

"*Je veux que tu me baises ici*," she said, wiggling her ass at me.

I wasn't going to turn that down. I walked over to her, taking the time to admire the view. As I reached her, however, I couldn't stop another image flashing across my mind. Nami in the same position, her hard nipples brushing against the cool metal, back arched in obvious invitation.

I frowned, pushing thoughts of Nami out of my head. I needed to focus on...shit. I couldn't remember her name. Now that I thought about it, had I even gotten her name? Oh well. It wasn't like I was planning some sort of relationship with her. *Ma chérie* would work just fine. There were three things people always needed to know how to say in other languages: Where is the bathroom? Do you speak English? And at least one endearment.

Thanks to her attention in the car, my cock was hard and ready, and as I slid my hand down her ass and between her legs, I found her soaking wet. I slid a finger inside her, then a second, earning a small moan. She pushed back against my fingers as I pumped them into her a couple times before pulling them out. She made a sound of protest, but I ignored it as I reached into my pocket and pulled out a condom. I'd make this one quick and then we could head inside and find out how long it'd take her to get me hard again. I doubted any of the things she'd talked about before were illegal here.

I opened my pants, pushing them down just low enough to get my cock free and rolled on the condom.

"Ready, *ma chérie*?" I asked as I pulled aside the flimsy fabric of her panties, exposing her bare skin.

"*Oui.*" She spread her legs even further apart. "Fuck me. *Se il vous plaît.*"

I rubbed the tip of my cock across her entrance, then pushed inside. She let out a string of French obscenities as I stretched her wide. I might've only been on the high end of average when it came to length, but I was thick and it always took a bit of work to get inside. By the time I was balls deep, her breath was coming in pants mixed with sounds of pleasure.

I slid my hands up from her hips, across her ribs and then around to cup her breasts. My hands covered them completely and I couldn't help but remember what Nami's had felt like, the weight of them. My grip tightened for a moment and then I began to move.

I started with a few shallow thrusts, letting my partner get used to the feel of me as I played with her nipples. The tips were long, perfect for me to tease, but they didn't feel quite right between my fingers. A flare of anger went through me. Anger at Nami for leaving. Anger at myself for not being able to forget.

I straightened, grabbing on to the girl's hips. The first time I slammed into her, she let out a surprised squeal. The second stroke was just as hard as the first and she swore, pushing back against me, wordlessly asking for more. All of the pent-up

7

frustration from the last two weeks exploded and I began to pound into her, taking her as fast and hard as I dared.

She dropped to the hood of the car, working one of her hands beneath her to rub her clit. Her bare flesh squeaked against the metal, mixing with the moans falling from her lips. I barely registered any of it. All I could think about was the wet heat of her, the way she was tight around me. I needed to come, to lose myself in the oblivion that only an orgasm could give me.

I didn't last long. I felt her start to come, her muscles tightening around me, milking me and I exploded. I groaned, biting back the name I wanted to call out. I closed my eyes, wanting to see only darkness, but it was Nami's face I saw. I opened my eyes as I took a step back, panting heavily.

I didn't look at her as I pulled off the condom and tossed it into the nearby garbage can. I heard the click of her heels as she walked over to me and I forced myself to smile at her. Her fair skin was flushed, her nipples swollen. She was beautiful, but not enough to completely distract me. I needed something more than just a quickie.

"Would you like something to drink?" I asked as I tucked myself back into my pants. I didn't bother doing up the zipper or buttons, however. I wasn't planning on wearing them much longer. Either she'd be leaving and I'd head to bed, or we'd be fucking again. Neither option required pants.

"Champagne?" she asked.

I nodded. "I think there's a bottle or two somewhere in the kitchen."

She smiled as she moved closer. Her hand slid down the front of my pants and I sucked in a breath as she cupped my sensitive flesh. She leaned forward and took my bottom lip between her teeth, lightly biting down before running her tongue across it to soothe away the sting.

"We fuck again, yes?" she asked as she took a step back, breaking our contact.

There was one decision made. "Yes," I said. "As many times as we can." I gave her a more genuine smile.

She smiled back and licked her bottom lip. "Good. I want to suck your dick next."

In spite of – or perhaps because of – her crude words, my cock gave an interested twitch as I thought of what it would feel like to slide into her mouth. Unbidden, the memory came to me of Nami on her knees in a storage room.

"This way." I reached out and took her hand.

A plan quickly formed in my head. The kitchen had counters that would be a perfect height for me to get my mouth on her. Then we'd head to the living room where she could return the favor while I sat on the couch. We could fuck there too. If I thought I could get it up again, we'd go to the bedroom.

As we walked into the kitchen, she spoke, *"En passant, mon nom est Cosette."*

Cosette, I thought. Nice name, but I doubted I'd remember it. She was just another fuck, after all.

Chapter 2

Reed

The body next to mine snuggled closer to me, her arm flung across my chest, breasts pressed against my side. As I headed towards wakefulness, I kept my eyes closed, trying to cling to the fantasy that it was Nami stretched out next to me. The closer I got to being fully conscious, however, the more my brain registered all of the things that were wrong.

The woman at my side was too tall. Her head was at my shoulder, her feet even with mine. And she was too thin. I could feel her ribs under my palm as it slid across her side. Her breasts and hips were smaller, her hair shorter and not curly.

Right. The blond from the club in Marseille. What was her name again? I know she'd told me after we'd fucked in the garage, but by the time she'd had her mouth around my cock, I'd forgotten it. She hadn't seemed to notice though. She'd definitely been an enthusiastic lover. By the time we'd passed out, I'd lost count the number of times we'd come and the number of places we'd fucked.

I should've been able to get what I'd wanted: a couple hours where I wasn't thinking about Nami. Instead, no matter what we'd done, I'd kept comparing her to Nami. How the two of them felt different. The sounds they'd both made.

I'd loved listening to Nami when we'd had sex. The moans. The little exclamations in her native language. How she'd cried out my name.

The blonde hadn't done that. She'd said things in French, but I'd understood the language almost as much as I did my own. Her cries of pleasure had been sharp, shrill. She'd said my name, but the accent hadn't been the same. She'd been adventurous and had clearly enjoyed the things I'd done to her, but I hadn't felt the responsiveness I'd gotten from Nami.

Claudia? I thought as I finally opened my eyes and looked down at her. No, it was something from a movie. Wait, not a movie, a play. A book? All three. Cosette. I'd had to take a couple shareholders to the theater once and we'd seen *Les Misérables*. I hadn't really cared for it, but I wasn't a big fan of musicals. The girl who'd played Cosette had been cute though.

I carefully extricated myself from under Cosette's arm and pulled the covers over her before heading across the hall to the bathroom. I turned on the shower and then, after a momentary internal debate, locked the bathroom door. I didn't want Cosette waking up when she heard the shower and deciding to join me. I didn't want to sound cold, but I was done with her. We'd had our fun and I'd let her use the shower when I was done if she wanted. I'd pay for her cab ride home and tell her I'd enjoyed our night together, but I didn't want her to think there was anything more to it than last night. The thought of her wet, naked body didn't turn me on now. It just made me tired.

I washed quickly even though I would've preferred to linger. I wasn't going to be an ass though and leave Cosette sitting in my room alone, wondering what she was supposed to do next. And I certainly wasn't going to make her think she had to call her own cab and pay her way home. I might not have been interested in her anymore, but I wasn't a complete cad.

I wrapped my towel tightly around my waist and wished I would've thought to bring clothes with me. I hadn't though, which meant I had to go back into my bedroom to find something to wear. Cosette was awake and smiled when I came in. She was still under the covers, and didn't seem like she was trying to seduce me, so that was good.

I spoke before she could say or do anything that would make this a whole lot more complicated. "The bathroom's free. Towels are in the little cabinet next to the shower."

Her smile wavered a bit, but she didn't get angry, so I kept going.

"I'll call a cab while you're cleaning up."

I saw a flash of anger in her eyes, and then it was gone. Without a word, she climbed out from under the covers and walked out. I breathed a sigh of relief that there hadn't been a fight. That was one of the reasons I usually didn't let my partners spend the night. Leaving right after sex was a lot less awkward than a morning-after conversation. I supposed it was something about the intimacy of literally sleeping together that made some women assume that there was more between us than sex.

I dressed quickly, unsure how long Cosette would be. She might take her time, hoping I'd change my mind, or she might be so pissed that she didn't want to be around me any longer than she had to. As soon as I pulled my shirt over my head, I called information for the number of the closest cab company.

Fortunately for me, the car arrived in record time and when Cosette came out of the bedroom, again dressed in her little handkerchief of a dress, I was able to escort her right out to the car. The driver gave me a knowing wink, but didn't say a word as Cosette climbed into the backseat, deliberately opening her legs so that I could see she wasn't wearing her thong. I really hoped she hadn't left it in my room, thinking she'd call about it later. I hated women who tried sneaky things like that.

I'd made no promises to her, no indication that I wanted a relationship. In fact, I'd specifically told her that all I wanted was a hook up. If she'd read anything else into it, it was on her. If she had left her panties in my room, they were going straight into the trash. As good as the sex had been last night – and considering how many times we'd done it, I couldn't really describe it as less than that – I was starting to have regrets.

As I watched the cab drive away, I ran my hand through my still-wet hair, sending droplets of water raining down on my shoulders. It was longer than I usually let it get. It was nearly impossible to tame unless I kept it short and, in those last couple weeks back home, it had been my private rebellion. Now it was a combination of that and just being lazy.

I went back inside. My stomach growled as I walked into the kitchen, but I couldn't find anything appetizing enough to eat. Finally, I grabbed a box of cereal and headed into the living room, fully intending to eat directly from the box and watch tv until I figured out what I was going to do now.

I thought I'd been lost before, drifting from one party to the next, one woman to the next. I'd had no direction, no idea of what the future held. That feeling had increased tenfold since I'd watched Nami walk out of my hotel room. I'd been living in the moment with her, but it somehow hadn't felt like that. If I was honest with myself, I'd felt more myself than I had...ever.

There'd been no plan, no schedule, but I'd taken charge, deciding what we were going to do, where we'd go. When we'd talked, I'd felt like I could share everything with her. She could have helped me figure out my path, I thought. She would've listened when I'd given her a list of ideas of what I wanted to do with the rest of my life, and she would've given an honest opinion. She would have supported whatever decision I made.

I leaned my head on the back of the couch and closed my eyes. For the first time since she'd left, I gave myself permission to call up the image of her face. Dark brown curls, cropped short. Just long enough to bury my fingers in the silky strands. Dusky skin. High cheekbones and a straight nose. Cyan eyes contributed to her exotic beauty. Only...it was more than her appearance. It was the way her full lips had curved into a smile. The blue-green sparkle of her eyes when she laughed.

A pang of longing went through me, so sharp that it was an almost physical hurt. I missed her, I finally allowed myself to admit. I missed her body, her scent. The intelligence of her conversation. The way I'd kept making a fool of myself in front of her.

I opened my eyes and looked around. The villa was just as beautiful as it had always been, every piece of furniture and decoration carefully chosen by a well-paid interior designer to show off the proper mixture of wealth and taste. I'd never really cared about any of that before, but it had been more of a not caring brought about by being used to it. Now, I saw things differently.

What was the point of all this, I asked myself. Why have all this money if all I was ever going to be was miserable? I didn't know if my parents were happy with their lives, but I doubted it. I knew Rebecca wasn't. She'd always pretended to be, but no one that nasty could be anything less than miserable with themselves. And then there was me. I'd never really thought about happiness before. It was all duty and loyalty. I'd tried to be happy with Piper, but even that hadn't done it.

I was tired of this, I realized suddenly. All of it. Not only tired of traveling around Europe without any purpose, fucking whoever I got into bed, and then moving on to the next party. I was sick of being a Stirling, of the responsibilities my last name put on my shoulders. Or, more accurately, the responsibilities my parents thought being a Stirling meant. I was tired of being told what to do, who to love and how I should behave.

I wanted more out of life than one party after another, one faceless woman. More than the power and money that came with being in charge of the Stirling businesses. I wanted my own life, but not because I wanted to rebel against my parents. I wanted it because I actually wanted to be happy.

And I was sure I needed Nami for that. My time with her had been the best I'd had for as long as I could remember. Even when I'd talked about my parents and my life back in Philadelphia, it hadn't seemed as important as it had before. When I was with her, I wanted to be a better man, not to impress anyone or make my parents proud. I wanted to deserve her. And not because she was a princess, but because of the amazing person I knew her to be. She deserved every happiness, and I wanted to give that to her.

I just didn't know if I was part of the equation. For all I knew, she was happy back in her home country, preparing for her upcoming wedding, ready to take on the mantle of crown princess. Despite her assertion that she'd always remember me, I couldn't help but wonder if I'd already faded from her mind. The thought hurt more than I cared to admit.

Chapter 3

Nami

I'd lied.

I'd told my parents that I'd submit to their will when I returned from Italy, but that promise had lasted all of two days before I'd given up.

It wasn't that I didn't love Saja. My island home was just far enough into the ocean that we didn't have to worry much about people from the mainland disturbing our peace. Every once in a while, we had visitors, but we weren't a country that thrived on tourism. Actually, we mostly kept to ourselves. While we imported goods, we weren't reliant on any one country, which allowed us to stay out of political issues. The beaches were beautiful, some rocky, some sandy. Our capital was more of a town than a city, but it was the closest thing to a metropolitan area we had. All of our businesses were there. Banks, police department, all of that. And, of course, the courthouse. We were a monarchy, but we used a justice system similar to America and the United Kingdom. The king or queen – whichever happened to be the ruling monarch at the time – did have the final say, but appeals rarely went that high. Our crime rate was low, our economy flourishing, and everything was perfect.

Everything except my life. Saja was my home. I loved it, just like I loved my family. King Raj and Queen Mara. My family had been ruling Saja for several generations, the crown past down from oldest child to oldest child, regardless of gender. And now it was my turn.

I was only twenty-two years-old, out of college for only a couple weeks, and my life was over. I opened my eyes, squinting against the early afternoon light. My head was pounding and my mouth was dry. There was a stale, nasty taste that told me, as much as the headache, that I'd drunk too much last night. Again.

When I'd left Princeton with my political science degree, I'd known what was coming next. An arranged marriage to a man of my parents' choice. Additional lessons in various foreign languages as well as ongoing updates on the political and economic situations in major world powers. Invitations to parties I didn't want to attend, mingling with people I didn't want to know. Basically, all the shit that came with me being the heir to the throne.

I hadn't been happy about it, but I'd accepted it as being just the way it was. I'd been thrilled with my parents' graduation gift of a European trip, but even that had been all about politics. Being in the right place at the right time. And, of course, behaving myself. I'd done my little bit of rebellion, though. Cut my hair...and lost my virginity. The first, everyone could see and my parents could brush under the table as some sort of fashion statement. The second had to be kept a secret.

Saja wasn't some backwards country where I'd be beaten or killed for having sex, but being the crown princess meant that my future husband would want to ensure that it was his child who would be next in line. That meant my parents, myself and the two bodyguards who'd been with me since I first went to America for college, all had to sign documents stating that I was a virgin.

I grinned despite the throbbing in my temples. That ship had sailed back in Princeton when I'd slept with my best friend. It hadn't meant anything though. My smile disappeared and I climbed out of bed. I didn't want to think about who I'd slept with next. I'd been trying to put those thoughts out of my head since I'd gotten back.

When I walked out of my bathroom, feeling a bit better after a quick shower and brushing my teeth, I noticed what I hadn't before. I hadn't been alone in my bed.

Fuck. I scowled. Who had I slept with last night? I closed my eyes, trying to remember. Most of the last two weeks was a blur. An intoxicated blur.

I'd played the dutiful daughter for two days, but then my parents had told me that they were down to their top three choices for my future husband. That hadn't been a surprise, but then I'd made the mistake of asking if I could meet all three and have the final say. I knew my parents loved me, but the look on their faces had made me hate them for a moment. It had been clear, without a word needed, that my marriage wasn't any of my concern.

I'd known that, of course, and if it hadn't been for what had happened in Paris, I might not have cared. I'd prepared myself. But then I'd met Reed and had experienced a glimpse of the kind of life I could've had. That taste of freedom had infected me and I couldn't seem to get back the same sense of duty I'd once had.

I wanted more out of life.

To my parents' dismay and disappointment, that meant I'd decided to have some fun. The first night, I'd only snuck out and gone to a club. I hadn't known until Kai and Tomas had shown up that my parents had a GPS tracker on my phone. Apparently, that's how my bodyguards had found me in Venice too, except the reception there had been so bad that it had taken them a while.

I pushed those memories aside. I didn't want to think about Venice.

My parents had freaked about my trip to the club, but the family's PR person, Mikkels, had managed to keep it under wraps. Then they'd doubled my guard detail. I could barely go to the bathroom without tripping over one of them.

The body on the bed rolled over and now I could see his face.

Right. Ari. Now I remembered. Well, pieces of it anyway.

Ari was only a couple years older than me and my newest bodyguard. I smirked. He'd done a hell of a lot more than guard my body last night. The flashes of memory I was getting involved a couple bottles of Saja's finest alcohol and a very naked man.

I glanced at the clock. Tomas and Kai would be back shortly, and there was no way Ari wasn't fired. It had been his job to keep me from doing anything stupid. Unfortunately for him, I was smarter than he was.

Since I'd been put under virtual house arrest, I hadn't been able to get out, but I'd managed to find enough alcohol in the house to keep me pleasantly buzzed every night. When I'd met Ari, however, something snapped. I didn't just want to annoy my parents, I wanted to piss them off.

Ari tossed off the blankets, revealing a toned, muscular body. He was shorter than Tomas and Kai, just under six feet, and thinner than them, but he couldn't exactly be called lean. His hair was dark and thick, his shoulders broad. He had strong, masculine features, hazel eyes and didn't resemble Reed in the slightest.

Which is exactly why I'd wanted to have sex with him. I'd needed someone who didn't look like Reed. Someone who would help me forget him. I'd told Reed that I wanted to remember him, and a part of me wanted to hang on, but I'd also learned how painful remembering could be. It might've been easier if it had just been sex, but there had been a connection with Reed I simply couldn't deny.

While I still didn't want to even think about someone chosen by my parents touching me, fucking me, I knew I couldn't keep reliving the memory of my time with Reed. It hurt too much. I needed him out of my head if I could ever go through with this. With the marriage, with training to become queen.

I shook my head. Apparently, last night hadn't worked.

I looked at Ari again, letting my eyes moved down from his chest to where his cock rested on his leg. I was happy to see a used condom on the bed

24

next to him – I hadn't been able to remember if we'd used one – but my attention quickly focused on the thick shaft slowly swelling as I watched.

"Good morning." Ari's voice was thick with sleep, drawing my attention back up to his face.

I smiled, but didn't say anything. It was clear on his face that he hadn't come to the realization he was completely screwed, and I didn't intend to change that. In fact, I was thinking I might want to at least give him something good to remember after he was fired. I walked towards him, putting a little extra swing into my step. I hadn't bothered to dress and his eyes watched the sway of my breasts as I walked towards him, his cock stiffening with each step.

His hand went towards it automatically and I watched him stroke himself as his cock grew. It wasn't quite as big as Reed's, but big enough to do the job. I climbed up the bed, enjoying the way his eyes were drawn to my breasts. I stopped between his legs and pulled his hand off of his cock.

"My turn." I grinned at him. I wrapped my hand around him and began to stroke, enjoying the feel of his skin beneath my palm.

"Princess," he groaned.

I saw something flicker across his eyes as he said the title and immediately tightened my hold. He swore and his eyes rolled back. At any moment he could realize this hadn't been a good idea after. I used my free hand to grab a condom from the side table and ripped it open with my teeth. I rolled it down his shaft, then moved up so I was straddling his waist.

His eyes darkened with lust as he reached up to my breasts. I waited for my body to respond to him the way it had done to Reed, but while his touch was pleasant, there was none of the heat I'd experienced before. I closed my eyes and sank down on his cock, letting out a breath as my body adjusted to him. His hips jerked as I settled and a ripple of pleasure went through me as the motion pressed him against that spot inside.

"Princess." His voice was strained.

"Shh." I shook my head. I didn't want to hear him talk, especially if he was going to call me "princess". I didn't want to be the princess. I wanted to be Nami.

I rocked back and forth, feeling the difference between Reed and Ari. I didn't know what it was, but it just didn't feel the same. I pushed the thought from my mind. I didn't want to think about Reed right now. I concentrated on the friction as I moved, the feel of his hands on my breasts.

As I began to move faster, Ari's hands dropped to my hips, not trying to move me, but just resting there. I opened my eyes, trying not to sigh in frustration. I couldn't remember if he'd been this passive last night, but this definitely wasn't doing it for me. I kept one hand on his stomach and moved the other to the place where our bodies joined. My fingers quickly found my clit and began the familiar back and forth motion I used to get myself off.

His fingers flexed on my hips and he groaned, his face flushing as I felt him come. Damn. I would've thought he'd had more stamina. I ground down against him, putting near painful pressure on my clit until the pressure burst inside me.

My nails dug into his stomach and he let out a gasp of pain.

"I'm sorry," I said, opening my eyes.

"It is quite all right, Princess." Ari panted. "I am here to serve."

The words hit me with an almost physical force. Here to serve. I was his princess. Even if he wanted me, I was still the princess first. Not a woman. Not a person. Just the princess.

I climbed off of him and went into the bathroom without a backward look. I knew when I came back out, he'd be gone, either fired or attempting to explain himself to Tomas and Kai. Either way, I wouldn't see him again. Not that it mattered. It hadn't worked.

I was keeping my promise to my parents even though the thought of doing so broke my heart. I wanted Reed.

Chapter 4

Reed

"Where the hell did you go, Nami?" I muttered to myself as I flopped back onto the couch.

One would think in the age of the internet, finding the king and queen of a country shouldn't be too difficult. I had no clue which country I was looking for, but I'd figured I'd start by searching the names she'd said. King Raj and Queen Mara. I'd found nothing.

Had she lied about who she was?

The thought had been circling in my mind for the past two days as I'd searched for her. I'd successfully ignored it up until now, but I'd known that I would have to face it at one time or another. Actually, I admitted, I'd hoped I wouldn't have to face it at all. I'd had this foolish notion that I'd be able to find her in just a few short hours, hop on a plane and go find her. The question would be unimportant.

But I hadn't found her. I'd gone to bed frustrated last night and it looked like I was going to do the same tonight. Now I had that question too.

Was the reason I couldn't find her because she wasn't a princess? Had she just made everything up in order to get rid of me? It seemed a bit extreme as far as plans went. She could've just said she was married or something like that. Married to some rich guy who insisted on the bodyguards. That wouldn't have been so far-fetched. Claiming to be a princess...now that one was a bit extreme.

She had to have been telling me the truth. I just couldn't figure out why I couldn't find her parents. Maybe I wasn't going about it the right way. I frowned at the laptop. I was a businessman. I knew how to read stocks and the business page. I knew a bit about researching things, but that was pretty much limited to typing stuff into a search engine and spending hours wading through shit. I'd been a CEO. Stuff like that was why I'd had assistants.

I glanced at the clock on my computer. It was night here but still evening back home. I'd resigned my position at the company, but I still had a good relationship with a lot of people back there, including one of my former assistants. Louis had been with me since the beginning, my first hire when I'd taken over as CEO five years ago. He was a couple years older than me, but had never behaved as if I was too young to be in charge.

I pulled my cell phone out of my pocket and scrolled down to Louis's number. He answered on the second ring.

"Mr. Stirling!" He sounded surprised, but pleased. "How are you doing?"

"Good, Louis," I said. "And I'm not your boss anymore, so please call me Reed."

"You're just on a sabbatical, Mr. Stirling." Louis's voice was firm. "How can I help you?"

A sabbatical. That was interesting. It appeared my parents hadn't told them that I'd actually resigned. It made sense though. A lie like that would be the best way to keep our shareholders from getting too nervous with Rebecca in charge. It wasn't a surprise that I hadn't heard the story before. I hadn't looked at any business news since leaving Philadelphia.

I wasn't about to correct Louis's mistaken impression. Best to speak to my parents first. With Louis, I stuck with what I needed. "I'm looking for someone. Twenty-two. Princess Nami Carr. Parents King Raj and Queen Mara. I need to know where Nami is from. Which country her parents are king and queen of."

If Louis thought this was an odd request, he didn't say anything about it. "Is this personal or business, Sir?"

"Personal." I definitely didn't want him doing this on business time. The last thing I needed was my sister finding out that I was looking for someone, not to mention that, no matter what my parents said, I wasn't in charge anymore. "I know that cuts into the amount of time you can spend searching."

"I'll do my best," Louis promised. There was a moment of silence, and then he added, "Do you know when you'll be coming back, Mr. Stirling?"

"No." I kept the answer simple even though I felt bad about essentially lying to him. I didn't have a plan to go back any time soon, if ever.

"I'll keep you apprised of what I find," he said. "Good night, Sir."

I hung up the phone and tossed it onto the couch next to me. I had absolutely no idea what to do now. Should I keep on with my feeble attempts to search or had I pretty much exhausted all of those options? I wasn't even really sure what I was looking for, or what I planned to do when I found it.

If I managed to track down her parents and figure out what country she was from, what then? I had vague notions of some sort of romantic reunion where I'd show up and convince her to give me a shot. I'd charm her parents, show them that I was the right match for their daughter. I was the one who deserved to marry –

Fuck.

I sat up and put my head in my hands. What was I thinking? I didn't want to get married again, especially not to someone I barely knew. I'd done that once and it hadn't ended well at all.

But Nami wasn't Britni. They were as different in personality as they were in looks, which basically meant night and day. Britni was spoiled, petty and arrogant. Nami wanted nothing more than to be a normal person, to live a normal life. She was kind and funny and sweet. She had a streak of steel in her too. A strength of which I didn't think even she knew the depth. I hadn't loved Britni, but Nami...

Dammit!

I slammed my hand on the coffee table. I wasn't in love with Nami. I couldn't be. Not after just a couple days. The problem was, I couldn't come up with another reason as to why she was constantly on my mind. It couldn't be explained away with only lust. I'd had other women who could've quenched it if that's all it was. Not that I didn't want her. It was stronger than lust though. I couldn't even rightly call it desire. It was a need, like food or water or air.

But it wasn't love, I told myself again. I'd thought before that I'd been in love and I'd been wrong. I wasn't going to make that mistake again. No, I'd wait until I found her, see if she was even willing to see if there was anything more to what we had than two nights of passion.

I was still arguing with myself regarding whether or not I was in love with Nami when my phone rang. I sighed when I saw the screen. Mom. I wasn't really in the mood to talk to her, but I'd ignored her previous two calls. Ignoring this one would just be rude.

"Mom." I tried to keep my voice flat. "How are you doing?"

"We're fine," my dad answered.

Right. Conference call.

"Reed, you need to come home."

My heart skipped a beat at the tone of my mother's voice. There was a hint of something that sounded a lot like panic.

"What's wrong? Is someone hurt? Sick?"

"It's Rebecca." The words were tight.

My heart constricted painfully. I might not have liked her very much, but she was my sister and I loved her for that.

"She's okay." My mom must've sensed that my father's terse statement made things sound bad.

"Physically," Dad said.

This couldn't be good.

"Your sister's in a bit of a...delicate situation."

I wished they'd just get on with it and tell me what was going on.

I heard my father's half-laugh at my mother's words. "Don't sugarcoat things, my dear. Reed, your

34

sister's been having an affair with Benjamin Westmore."

My first thought popped out of my mouth. "Seriously? He's older than both of you."

"Not Senior," my dad said. I could almost hear him rolling his eyes. "Junior."

"Right." I felt stupid. "And he's married."

"Married with kids," Mom clarified.

"And to make matters worse, Westmore Senior has already sent us invitations to the wedding of his youngest son, Blayne."

I'd only known Blayne Westmore by reputation, but I had to admit that I was surprised he'd settled down at all. I also had the vague recollection that my parents had been trying to marry him to my sister. That would make tensions between the two families run a bit high.

"So don't go to the wedding," I suggested. "Send an expensive gift."

"We're not calling for advice." Dad sounded annoyed. "We want you to come home and take the third invitation. Go with us."

I stood up and began to pace. I couldn't sit still and listen to this. "You want me to fly all the way home for the wedding of someone I don't know."

"We want you to show everyone that we're a united family and that we will rise above this little...incident."

My mom, ever the diplomat.

"I'll think about it." I couldn't bring myself to refuse outright. The sense of duty to family did run deep. "But I'm not making any promises."

"We'll have a ticket reserved for you on Friday if you're coming."

After a couple more moments of small talk, the call ended. I knew they were both frustrated that I hadn't made any promises, but I'd given them the best I could. Besides, I had Nami to think of. I needed to find her before it was too late and she was married.

I paused, sighing. If it wasn't too late already.

I had no idea how fast things like this moved in her country. For all I knew, she could've gone straight from the airport to her wedding. Time wasn't on my side.

However, I thought, being back in the States might give me more resources. I could hire a private investigator to find Nami, deal with him face-to-face instead of making calls from halfway around the world.

I would do it, I decided. I'd go home. Something inside me clicked. This was a turning point, I thought suddenly. Whatever happened, it was going to happen at home because once I'd found Nami – or was told that finding her wasn't possible – I would have to decide where to go from there. There would be no putting it off anymore. My weeks of fun were over and it was time to start looking towards the future. A future I hoped Nami would be a part of.

Because, no matter what I told myself, I was in love with her.

Chapter 5

Reed

When my parents had called to try to coax me into coming home, I'd thought they'd exaggerated how bad things were. By the time I arrived in Philadelphia a few days later, things were even worse. Rebecca had driven our company into the ground. Money was missing. Clients were jumping ship and the only thing that had saved the employees was Julien Atwood.

I could feel my parents watching me as my father explained that Julien had convinced his family into buying out the company at a loss. The papers had been signed yesterday. I knew why they were watching. It had been Julien, after all, who'd gotten the girl, but I didn't begrudge him Piper. In fact, I was happy for her, for them both. They'd been able to overcome so many obstacles to be together, not the least of which was their families and pasts. I could only hope to be so lucky.

"How bad is it?" I asked, pulling myself out of my thoughts.

My father frowned at his plate. "We have other assets," he said. "Other sources of income."

I knew what he meant. Stocks and real estate mostly. I also knew how lavishly my family lived. The business had been a steady source of income they'd been able to spend without risking their net worth.

"It's not only the money," Mom spoke up. "What happened with Rebecca and Benjamin, and then the Atwoods having to buy us out..." She shook her head. "Our societal standing has never been more precarious." She gave me a disapproving look. "And all because of that Piper girl."

I leaned back in my chair, no longer hungry. "I'm not with Piper, Mom," I reminded her.

"Do you think that makes it any better?" Dad asked. "The whole Brock scandal overshadowed what happened between you and Britni, but people didn't completely ignore the fact that you left the daughter of a prominent family for a whore. Now she's with the Atwood boy and you look like a fool."

"Piper isn't a whore," I snapped. I wasn't sure which part of that pissed me off the most. The fact that he'd referred to Brock Michaels being arrested for rape to be a 'scandal' or that his concern over

40

Piper choosing Julien over me had nothing to do with whether or not I was hurting.

"Stripper, sorry." He gave me a hard look that said he wasn't sorry at all.

"Why didn't you liquidate other assets to save the business?" I hadn't intended to ask the question, knowing it would come across as accusatory, but my patience had all but disappeared with my father's statements.

His face flushed, a mottled red creeping up his neck. "I don't believe that's any of your business."

"You practically beg me to come back here and then tell me that it's not my business?" I crossed my arms. "What do you want from me?"

Both parents looked startled at the blunt question, but I didn't try to smooth it over. I was through waiting for and following their instructions like a good little puppet.

"Tell him." My mother's voice was soft.

Dad glared at her for a moment and then sighed. "I suppose you do need to know." He folded his hands on the table. "We seem to have gotten behind on some of our property taxes." He shifted in his seat. "And made some bad investments."

"So when you said you had other assets and income...?" I let the question trail off.

"We won't starve," he said. "But we're going to lose the villa, the vineyard and maybe the apartment. All sold to pay our taxes."

"Are you asking to move back here full-time?" I asked.

The house here on Chestnut Hill had originally belonged to my parents, but they'd sold it to me a couple years ago when I'd decided I preferred it to an apartment in the city. The family used it occasionally and I didn't mind as long as I was given advanced warning. I valued my privacy, particularly from my family.

"It may come to that," Dad said. "But I was thinking more about the stock you own."

"What about it?" My eyes narrowed. I had a bad feeling I knew where this was going.

"You're not majority holder, but you do own the second biggest chunk. I want you to buy out everyone else and get the business back from the Atwoods."

My mom reached across the table as if she was going to touch me, then stopped and pulled her hand back. "You've done well for yourself, Reed."

She was right. I had. While I did enjoy the comforts that my family name offered and I had like being able to stay at the villa and the vineyard in Italy, I had money beyond the trust fund I'd inherited when I'd turned twenty-one. I'd invested well and, while I had splurged on occasion, I didn't spend excessively. I'd promised myself that I would never count on my inheritance or trust fund to support me.

"What would you do with the business if I got it back?" I asked.

"Well, you're back now," Dad said. "And the stock would be in your name, of course. We always intended for you to inherit the company. It'd just come a bit early."

And there it was. Like the past few months hadn't even happened. I was expected to come back and pick up as if I hadn't been away at all. I'd had my fun and now I was supposed to be the good son again, regardless of what I wanted.

"I have a lot to think about." I pushed my chair back and stood. "You said the wedding's at one tomorrow?" My mother nodded. "I'll see you when it's time to go then."

Before either parent could press the matter any further, I walked out of the dining room, heading for the stairs. I'd wondered why my parents had insisted I come to my house rather than meeting them at their place. Now I knew why. It was a not-so-subtle way of letting me know that if I didn't let them stay here, they could be homeless.

I was so caught up in my thoughts that I almost ran into Rebecca.

"What are you doing here?" The question came out more harshly than I'd intended.

"Hiding," she snapped. "I'm a disgrace, or didn't our parents tell you?"

"Sorry," I apologized automatically. "You just startled me. I figured you'd be at your place."

"My place." She barked a bitter laugh. "I don't have a place, Reed. When Mom and Dad found out about the affair, they stopped paying my rent and I didn't have any choice but to live with them."

I searched her face, trying to tell if she knew what was happening with our parents' finances, but I couldn't see anything other than outrage at the indignities she'd supposedly suffered.

"And now that the golden child is back, I'll fade into the background again."

I knew I should feel some measure of sympathy for Rebecca considering how she had always been overlooked when it came to a lot of things, but I'd been just as much a pawn of our parents as she had. She could've done things differently, chosen to make something of herself separate from our family.

"I don't know if I'm staying," I admitted.

She rolled her eyes. "And why wouldn't you? You have everything here." A cruel smile curved her lips. "Well, everything except Piper. I hear she and Julien are quite the couple."

"I'm happy for them," I said quietly. Her expression said she didn't believe me, but I was telling the truth.

"Are you thinking of trying to get Britni back then?" she asked. "Because that ship sailed too."

"What's that supposed to mean?"

The smug look on her face said she'd been holding on to this particular tidbit. "She's engaged. Or will be soon enough from what I understand. Rich, good-looking, and here's the best part...he's not in love with another woman."

My hands wanted to curl into to fists, but I forced them to stay open. "You do know I never loved Britni, right? If she's found someone who loves her, good for her." My voice was even.

Anger flashed in her hazel eyes. Apparently, my lack of reaction annoyed her.

"Love's for idiots." She folded her arms over her chest and squared her shoulders. "Men marry for lust or money and women marry for money or prestige."

"Oh really?"

"Come on, Reed. You can't still seriously be that naïve."

"Is that what you were doing with Benjamin Westmore?" I asked. "Trying to get him to pay you off as his mistress?"

Her cheeks flushed. "That was a mistake. I've learned since then." She glanced at her watch, an expensive one I'd never seen before. "I have to go. Cecily's expecting me."

"Cecily Postman?"

Rebecca nodded. "We're spending the weekend together since I'm apparently not good enough to go to the Westmore wedding." She turned to start down the hall.

"Cecily's in London."

Rebecca froze. "What?"

"I saw her at the airport when I arrived. She was getting ready to board a plane to London and didn't say a word about you meeting her there." I took a step towards my sister. "Where are you really going?"

Her jaw tightened. "None of your business."

"Rebecca..." My voice held a note of warning.

"Let it go, Reed. It's my life."

Trying for the nice, protective older brother wasn't working, so I went for option number two. "Are you sleeping with Cecily's father?"

The stiffening of Rebecca's spine told me the answer before she spoke, "And if I am?"

"Then you're stupid, Rebecca. He's old enough to be your father. His daughter is your best friend, for crying out loud."

"Tell you what, Reed." She still didn't look at me. "You worry about your love life and I'll worry about mine."

"Well, I guess you get a point since this one isn't married."

She opened her mouth, then closed it.

There was nothing I could do but watch her walk away. She wouldn't listen to me, I knew. Rebecca never listened to anyone. She did what she wanted to do and that was that. I shook my head and resumed my walk to my room. I was seriously jet-lagged and if I didn't get some sleep, I wouldn't be even close to presentable for the wedding tomorrow.

It wasn't until my parents and I were in the car heading to the church when I realized I hadn't once thought about the fact that I was going to see Piper again. I'd been too preoccupied wondering if either Louis or the PI I'd hired had found anything on Nami. Once I was seated, however, I found myself scanning the crowd for Piper. Just before things got started, I spotted her with Julien. She looked at me and gave me a tight smile. I could tell, even from a distance, that she was worried how I'd react to seeing her with him. I smiled and nodded, then turned away, hoping she could still read me well enough to know that we were okay.

As soon as the wedding began, however, Piper was the furthest thing from my mind. I couldn't help but wonder if Nami was married already. Had her wedding been like this? When everyone turned to watch the bride walk down the aisle, I didn't see the tall blonde. In my mind's eye, it was Nami, expression politely resigned. Or had she been happy? Did her parents pick her a match she could love?

I wasn't sure which thought bothered me more. That Nami would be miserable with a man she didn't care for, or that she would fall in love with him. I barely heard the ceremony as I tortured myself with thoughts of Nami and her unknown betrothed. At their wedding. Holding hands. The kiss. Dancing. The wedding night.

I let out a breath. I had to believe that she wasn't married yet. It would be hard enough to convince her to break an engagement. She'd never divorce her parents' choice.

By the time I found myself at the same table with Piper and Julien, I'd all but convinced myself that it wouldn't matter what I did. I'd lost Nami the moment I'd let her walk out of the hotel. To my surprise, Piper seemed genuinely concerned for me and I found myself telling her and Julien everything. Part of me did it because I wanted Piper to know that I understood what she'd said when she'd chosen Julien over me and there were no residual feelings. Another part of me needed it for another reason. I had to tell someone about her, about what I was feeling.

When I finished, Piper leaned forward, her dark green eyes kind. She put her hand over mine in a sincere and platonic gesture. "Do you love her?"

I didn't let myself overthink it. "Yes."

"Then fight for her, Reed." She squeezed my hand. "If what the two of you have is real, don't you dare give up. You deserve to be happy."

I smiled at her and thanked her, but in the back of my head, I couldn't help but wonder if she was right. Did I deserve to be happy?

Chapter 6

Nami

After my little fling with Ari, I'd given up on using a man to make me forget what I'd lost. Actually, I'd given up forgetting at all. I'd worked so hard to remember Reed that it was impossible to erase him now. That realization had depressed me enough that I'd spent the last two days in bed, getting up only when necessary. Like to use the bathroom and find more alcohol. I knew my parents had forbidden anyone to bring me anything, but I had enough blackmail on Tomas and Kai now that they were willing to help me out in exchange for a promise that I wouldn't try to sleep with anyone else. Neither one of them had been happy that they'd had to fire Ari and make up a lie to tell my parents.

The door to my bedroom banged open, making me jump, then wince at the bolt of pain that went through my head.

"Enough!" My father's voice was loud and stern, neither of which did anything to help my headache.

I grabbed the covers and pulled them up over me even though I was fully clothed. "Ever heard of knocking?" I muttered.

"Nami!" My mother chastised me. "You cannot speak to your father that way."

I sighed and climbed out of bed. The room wavered a bit, but didn't spin, so I was able to stay on my feet. I considered that to be quite the accomplishment. "Sorry." I couldn't leave it at an apology though. "Just figured a warning might've been nice. I could've been changing my clothes."

"Considering you have not changed clothes for more than two days, I did not believe that would be an issue." My father raised an eyebrow.

He had a point.

"This behavior of yours must stop," Mother said. "It is not befitting any member of a royal family, much less the heir."

I looked from one to the other. I could see bits and pieces of myself in both of them. Halea looked nearly identical to our mother, but I was a blend of them in personality as well as physical appearance. I'd also inherited a stubborn streak from both of them.

"I'm staying inside," I said. "But don't worry, I'll make sure I'm presentable for any public stuff." I swayed and put my hand on the bedside table to steady myself. "And that's what matters, isn't it? The face we present to the public. It's not like I'm making any major decisions or anything."

"You are the crown princess," Father spoke through gritted teeth. "It is your duty to learn all these things regarding the rule of Saja."

I resisted the urge to roll my eyes. I was already testing my father's patience and I had a feeling it would've been the last straw. "Like I said, I'll make sure I'm the picture of perfection when we interact with the public. Let me have the privacy of my own room to do as I please."

"Namisa Persephone Carrmoni."

I flinched at the sound of my official name. Within the family, we never referred to each other by our birth names. Those were for public face only. All Saja royalty had two names, the one that went on records and treaties, that the media used, and the one we used within the privacy of our home and when we were moving about unofficially. I'd taken that a step further when I'd shortened my last name for school. Four years away at school as Nami Carr, I'd almost forgotten that other name.

"This will stop. Now."

I recognized my father's tone. It was the one he used when he was having the final say in something. Like he was now.

"There will be no more alcohol save for wine or champagne at official functions. You will not become intoxicated, either publicly or privately."

My hands curled into fists as he continued.

"You will retire to your room at a respectable time unless busy with state or family business. You will wake no later than seven, bathe, dress and make an appearance at breakfast. All attire will be from your approved wardrobe, and you will not deviate from that."

There was a moment of silence and then my mother spoke, her voice soft. "I know this is difficult to accept, Nami, but you are the princess, and it is your duty to take on these responsibilities. You have always known this would be the way."

I *had* known, but there was a difference between being a child, or even a teenager, thinking of being in my early twenties as so far away, and being here and now.

"I understand how difficult this is for you."

It was on the tip of my tongue to snap at her that she didn't know. She had married in to the throne. I had been raised for it. The only person who could've understood was my grandmother, my father's mom. She had ruled before him. But I couldn't ask her for advice or guidance. She'd passed away when I'd been only seven. I didn't say anything to my mother though. It would have been bad manners to remind

54

her that she was royal by marriage, not blood.

"It was a mistake to allow you to go to America for school," Father said. "There is a reason all Saja royals remain on the island for their schooling. Your roots are here, Nami, not out there."

"I know," I said softly. My headache was fading away, as were the other effects of what I'd drank, and a resigned depression was starting to sink in.

"So we are agreed?" Father asked. "No more of this foolishness?"

"We are agreed." I looked down, not wanting him to read on my face what I was feeling.

"Good," Mother said. "Now, make yourself presentable and join us in the receiving room. Wear the blue dress at the front of your closet."

I stiffened. I knew which dress she meant, and I knew why it had been purchased. "You've chosen?"

"We have," Father said. "Dress and join us. You will be meeting your future husband within the hour."

I watched them leave without any of us speaking again. When the doors closed behind them, I sank to my knees, all the strength running out of my legs. Here it was. My engagement. The fork in the road. Accepting this would mean I could fight it no more. My fate would be sealed.

I would've laughed at that if I could've ensured I wouldn't cry instead. My fate had been sealed the moment I'd been born, then again when my brother had died. I didn't have a choice other than how I would enter in to this. I could drag my feet, fight it tooth and nail, and still lose, or I could be gracious and hope that the man my parents had chosen was good and kind.

But first, I had to take a shower, because there was no way I was going to meet my fiancé smelling like someone who'd been sleeping off a bender under a bridge. Then I would dress and go to the receiving room to meet the man with whom I'd be spending the rest of my life.

The blue dress my mother had purchased while I was away was a little loose even though it was technically my size. I frowned. I must've lost weight over the past couple weeks. Not surprising. I hadn't really been consuming much real food recently. I smoothed it down, making a couple little adjustments here and there until it fit well enough. I smoothed down my curls. They were still damp, but presentable. I went with minimum make-up and a pair of heels that gave me a couple inches but were still considered decent.

I gave myself one last look in the mirror. I could still see faint bruise-like smudges under my eyes, but they were only visible if someone paid close attention. I doubted anyone would notice. I took a deep breath, cleared everything else out of my mind and headed down the hallway. The receiving room was at the front of the palace, allowing us to bring people into our home without bringing them into the part where we actually lived.

When I walked inside, my parents were already there. Standing with them were three people. I recognized two of them as part of a fairly wealthy family. I couldn't remember their name, but it didn't surprise me that they were the ones my parents had picked.

"May we present our eldest daughter, Namisa Carrmoni," Father spoke in our native language.

I bowed my head a bit, enough to indicate respect, but without making it seem like they were above me. The woman curtsied, but I saw her pale eyes watching me. There was no doubt in my mind that she was wondering how long it would be before I'd give her a grandchild to assure her bloodline on the throne. Her husband bowed and kept his head down, his face carefully guarded. He was smart. I wasn't sure if that was a good thing or a bad thing.

I let my eyes turn to the third person now. He'd bowed, but not as low or as long as his father, and he hadn't kept his head down. His eyes were a clear blue, the kind that had the potential to be as cold as a glacier. Right now, they were unreadable as they met mine. He smiled, but it didn't reach his eyes. He was handsome, with jet black hair and chiseled features. When he straightened, I saw that he was about average height, a bit under six feet tall, and muscular, with wide, broad shoulders. Most women would've been attracted to him. If I hadn't had Reed on my mind, I might've been too.

"Princess Namisa, meet Machai and Naomi Nekane, and their son Tanek." Mother's voice was stiff and I wondered if she hadn't been as fond of this match as my father. "Tanek is your betrothed."

I'd figured as much, but hearing it said out loud like that still made my stomach flip, and not in a good way.

Tanek stepped forward as I extended a hand. He took it, bowed slightly and kissed the back of my hand. "Princess." His voice was low and cultured.

"Tanek."

Something dark passed across his eyes at my use of his first name. I tightened my jaw and lifted my chin. Too bad if he didn't like it. He didn't have a title and, until we were married, he wouldn't. Even then, I would still be above him. Others would be required to address him as prince, and then king, but I would still be the leader.

"We have decided that a short engagement would be best," Father said.

Mother turned to me, her expression tightly polite. "We have a lot to do, my dear, so we'll be spending every day until the wedding planning for the event."

I heard what she wasn't saying. I would have no chance to screw this up. They'd made their decision and now I had to live with it.

Chapter 7

Reed

Piper was right, I decided. I deserved to be happy and that couldn't happen until I knew where things stood with Nami. Even if she didn't want me, if she'd already married her guy, at least I'd know.

And no matter what happened, I was done here. Not just done with my family's business – which didn't belong to my family anymore – but with Philadelphia, with the obnoxious high society people, with everyone, related or not.

I wasn't going to do what my parents had asked and buy the company out from the Atwoods. Besides the fact that I wasn't interested in being in charge again, I didn't trust my family to do right by the people who worked there. I trusted Julien to though.

I laughed at that and shook my head as I looked down at the list I'd made. I was almost done. The last thing I had to do was tell my parents, and I was putting that off until I knew where I was going. I would eventually tell my parents, but I wanted to wait until I was ready to leave before I said anything. Give them less time to try to talk me out of it.

The first thing I'd done was pay ahead on property taxes for two years, and then sign the house over to my parents. It wasn't as hard as I thought it would be, giving away the place that had been my home pretty much my entire life. I guessed that was because it hadn't actually felt like my home. Not just mine. Even at my age, I'd always felt like I was still at my family's house, not mine. Now it was theirs again. I just hoped it would give my parents enough time to get their feet under them because I wasn't planning on bailing them out with anything else.

I'd had to pull quite a few strings to get everything together on a Sunday, but the Stirling name wasn't complete mud, especially when it was linked to my first name. Granted, people knew about the whole Britni thing, but the Michaels weren't exactly bright shining stars in Philly at the moment and business people were more likely to overlook an affair versus bad financial choices. It helped that what I was asking for had to do with money, and I had plenty.

Everything that was under my name was being turned into cash. I wouldn't be able to get it all today, but I'd set things into motion to have everything split into several different accounts at different banks. I'd taken a loss on some art work and on a couple other possessions, but getting this taken care of quickly meant more to me than a couple hundred thousand dollars. I wanted to be ready to go at a moment's notice.

I looked around the living room, realizing for the first time how nothing here was mine. The furnishings had changed a bit over the years, but I'd hired the same decorator my parents had used. There were family pictures on the wall, but they were all portraits or identical prints of ones in the apartment. I'd kept very few mementos over the years and none of them were displayed.

I didn't have anything I wanted to take with me. The knowledge that I could leave at any point with just my wallet and passport filled me with a sense of relief and a thrill of excitement.

A knock at the door pulled me from my thoughts and I got up. I wasn't sure who it could be. Rebecca was going to come visit me, but it might've been my parents. I didn't really want to see any of them, but I couldn't think of anyone else. Unless Piper and Julien had decided to stop by, but while we'd gotten along fine at the wedding, I didn't think we were at the 'drop by for a visit' stage.

When I opened the door, I almost slammed it shut again. The only thing that stopped me was the fact that I couldn't move. My feet were frozen to the spot and I was pretty sure my mouth was hanging open.

"Hey, Reed." Britni grinned up at me, her light blue-gray eyes sparkling. "Heard you were back in the city."

"Britni." I found my voice, and was relieved to hear it sounded normal.

"Aren't you going to invite us in?" Britni asked.

It wasn't until then that I realized she wasn't alone. The man behind her was about average in height and build. Sandy brown hair and pale green eyes. He was good-looking, I supposed, in an average sort of way. I assumed this was the new fiancé.

"Come in." I stepped out of the way and let Britni and her guy walk on by.

"This is Jeremy MacKenzie, by the way," Britni called over her shoulder. She waved her fingers at me, a giant diamond glinting in the light. "My fiancé. He just asked me tonight."

"Nice to meet you, Jeremy." A strange, surreal feeling had come over me. "And congratulations."

Britni went straight into the kitchen and started rooting around, coming up with a bottle of wine a few seconds later. Without asking permission, she pulled a couple of glasses out of the cupboard and poured us each a glass.

"I think we need a toast," she said, raising her glass. "To true love."

I was glad she hadn't said it after I'd taken a drink. I probably would've choked on it. As it was, I barely managed to swallow it despite how good it was. What the hell was she doing here?

"This is good, Reed." She gave me another smile. "Then again, you always did have good taste."

Jeremy gestured around the kitchen. "Did you hire someone or do it yourself?"

"Hired someone," I said. "But I don't think she did much in here. Looks pretty much the same as it did when I was a kid."

"You grew up here?" he asked.

I nodded. "On and off. We lived in the city too."

"Well, while you two are getting to know each other, I'm going to visit the restroom." Britni set down her glass and breezed out of the room.

"Is this as awkward for you as it is for me?" Jeremy asked, pitching his voice low so that Britni couldn't hear.

I let one side of my mouth curve up in a half smile. "I imagine so."

"I told her we shouldn't come," he said. "Especially not without calling first."

"Britni gets what Britni wants," I said wryly.

"She didn't get you," he observed.

"She did for a while," I countered. I grinned at

65

him. "But I got away."

"Rumor has it there was another woman involved." Jeremy slid closer, his voice taking on a conspiratorial tone. "A stripper?"

I rolled my eyes. "Not exactly the whole story."

"I didn't think so." He reached over and put his hand on my arm. "Arranged marriages usually have secrets. I know mine does."

I stared at his hand, my mind reeling. Was this seriously happening? I had to be reading into it, right? This was one of those platonic bromance moments, right?

"But when you have an understanding..." His hand slid up my arm and around the back of my neck.

Oh, shit.

I took a step back. "Sorry, Jeremy. I didn't mean to make you think..."

"No problem." He took a step back and held up his hands, palm out. "My mistake. I just assumed..."

"You two getting along?" Britni said as she came back into the kitchen. "My two boys?"

"I'm not your boy." I gritted my teeth. "What are you doing here, Britni?"

"And that's my cue to take a look at this beautiful house." Jeremy drained the last of his wine and walked out of the room.

"All right," I said as Jeremy disappeared. "Talk

to me."

"Can't a girl just want to see her ex-husband?" Britni gave me wide, innocent eyes.

I raised an eyebrow. "Do you really want me to replay the night I told you it was over?"

Her expression tightened for a moment, then relaxed. "I've had time to think about what happened between us and I want us to be friends."

"Friends?" I echoed. This had to be a dream. Some sort of weird, abstract dream.

"Of course." She moved in close, backing me against the counter before I knew what was happening. "Friends with benefits." She put her hand on my chest and slid it down between us.

I jumped to the side as she cupped my cock through my pants. "What the hell, Britni?!"

"Jeremy's parents want the same thing yours did. An heir. And as I'm sure you've already figured out, I'm not exactly his type."

"So get artificially inseminated," I snapped. "Because I'm not an option."

Britni gave me one of her pouts. "Come on, Reed. You can't say that we didn't have fun together."

"Fun?" I raised an eyebrow. "I don't know what your definition of fun is, but nothing I experienced during our marriage was fun."

She reached for the zipper at the front of her

shirt and pulled it down, exposing bare skin. "You didn't have any fun? That's disappointing." She opened her shirt and flashed her breasts. "What do you say we try again?"

"Zip up your shirt and tell me what the hell you're really doing here, because I know it's not because you want to fuck."

"Actually," Britni said. "It is." She walked towards me. "I want a baby. Your baby."

My eyes narrowed suspiciously. I hadn't heard much about the Michaels family since Brock went to jail, but what had happened couldn't have had a positive effect on their finances. Pieces fell into place, but I was hoping I was wrong. I didn't want to think Britni could be that manipulative and cold, but it made sense. If I got her pregnant, she could claim that the two of us had some sort of random night of passion. A simple paternity test and I'd be paying a hefty amount of child support. And she knew I wouldn't argue with it because I would never let a kid suffer.

"I think you need to leave."

She yanked up her zipper. "Are you fucking kidding me? After what you did to me? You owe me."

"I owe you? I signed the divorce papers and gave you more than the prenup allotted." My temper was rising and I fought to keep it down. "We're done,

Britni. In fact, I'm done with this whole fucking thing."

"What are you talking about?"

"I'm leaving," I snapped. "Everyone in this town is fucking crazy." So much for my carefully thought out plan to reveal my plans only after I was going. Oh, well. In for a penny... "I'm leaving Philadelphia, and once I'm gone, I'm not coming back."

She laughed, a shrill, brittle sound. "Sure you are. Everything you know is here. You're not going anywhere."

"Yes," I said firmly. "I am. "I've made all the arrangements. I'm just waiting on a call and then I'm gone."

"Darling." Jeremy spoke from the doorway. "I hate to be a bother, but my parents are expecting us so we can make the official family announcement."

Britni glared at me for a moment longer before fixing a fake smile on her face and beaming it at Jeremy. Based on his expression, he wasn't fooled. I had a moment to wonder what he was going to get out of this marriage. It wasn't like he really had to worry about getting outed. Being LGBT friendly was quite popular among our social circle and I hadn't heard that his family was overly religious.

"Let's go. I'm done here." Britni gave me another dirty look before stalking out of the room.

I followed them to the door to make sure they

left and when it closed, I stayed there, resting my forehead against the door for a moment. If I hadn't been certain that I was going to leave Philadelphia and not look back, what had just happened clinched things for me.

I really hoped someone found Nami soon, because if I had to stay here much longer, I was going to go crazy.

Chapter 8

Reed

I looked down at her as she kissed her way down my body, her mouth leaving a hot trail across my skin. They were wet, open-mouthed kisses, teeth and tongue alternating to sting and soothe. When she dipped her tongue in my bellybutton, I laughed and was immediately rewarded with a nip to my stomach.

I groaned. "You're killing me here, Princess."

Her hands slid up my thighs, fingers massaging the tight muscles there. I wondered how it was physically possible to feel tense and relaxed at the same time. Then again, it seemed like it was only during sex that it happened, and so many impossible things were possible when two people came together.

"Stay still," she whispered as she moved her head lower. She put her hand on my stomach and my muscles bunched and jumped under her palm.

How the hell did she expect me to stay still when her touch was like electricity? Whenever I was near her, it felt like every cell was trying to find a matching one in her body, its other half. The pull was beyond magnetic, beyond anything I'd ever felt before.

I sucked in a sharp breath as her tongue darted out to taste me. Her fingers danced over my swollen flesh and it twitched in response. My eyes wanted to close so I could focus solely on the sensation of her hot breath as she lowered her head. I forced them to stay open, wanting to watch her take me in her mouth.

Her lips slowly closed around the tip and I felt her tongue tease the skin there. I reached down and put my hand on her head. Her hair was like silk between my fingers and I wondered what it would feel like long, how the curls would brush against my thighs when she went down on me. Maybe I could talk her into growing it out.

My cock slid over her tongue as she took more and more of me. Her lips stretched impossibly wide as she neared the base. I couldn't take my eyes off her. She looked up at me as the head of my dick bumped against the back of her throat. I waited for her to gag, withdraw, and use her hand as she took the first couple inches again. Instead, she took a slow breath and let me slide down her throat.

"Fuck!" My back arched and it took all of my self-control not to thrust harder into her mouth. One hand tightened in her hair and the other grabbed on to the sheets.

Her nose brushed against my pelvic bone and she stayed there, my cock engulfed in the soft wet of her mouth. One hand moved beneath me, cupping my balls, then rolling them in her hand. After what felt like years, she raised her head and my cock fell out of her mouth with a near obscene plop. She used her free hand to stroke me as she ran her tongue along the underside of my shaft.

"Nami," I moaned her name as she took one of my balls into her mouth. The hand on my cock didn't miss a single stroke and I could feel my orgasm building deep inside.. I was so close. Her hands and mouth were doing such wonderful things that I never wanted her to stop, but the end was coming...

I jerked awake, disoriented for a moment as I tried to remember where I was and what I was doing. Right. I was at home. Or, at least, at the house on Chestnut Hill. That was home for now.

My phone rang again and I realized that's what had woken me. I fumbled for it, my brain and body still thick with sleep. I managed to get it just before it went to voicemail.

"Hello?"

73

"Mr. Stirling?"

I frowned at the familiar voice. I should know it, but couldn't quite place it. "Yes?"

"It's Louis."

Right, my former assistant. "Of course. Good morning." There was a reason he was calling me, but I couldn't for the life of me figure out what it was.

"You asked me to look into finding someone for you."

I sat up, all traces of sleep gone. "Did you find her?"

"I spent the weekend working with your PI like you asked and I'm pretty sure we found her."

My heart was pounding so hard against my chest that I thought Louis might be able to hear it. This was it.

"You said her name was Nami Carr, correct? And her parents were Raj and Mara, King and Queen of some country you didn't know."

"That's right."

"What we found is a Princess Namisa Carrmoni, daughter of a King Amir Rajada Carrmoni and Queen Persephone Mara Carrmoni."

I crossed my legs and rested my elbows on my knees. She hadn't given me a complete alias in an attempt to make it impossible for me to find her after all.

"From what Mr. Stiles and I found, the

Carrmonis are the royal family of a small island country called Saja. The family name has changed over the years since it seems like they don't follow a traditional monarchy of the eldest son taking the throne..."

"I don't want a history lesson, Louis," I said dryly. It took a great amount of self-control not to just yell at him to tell me how to get to Saja.

There was a moment of silence before Louis continued. "I've emailed you a picture of Princess Namisa. I'm confident this is the young woman of whom you spoke."

"And you said the name of the country is Saja?"

"It is."

"How do I get there?" I climbed out of bed and headed into the living room where I'd left my laptop on the table.

"I've included those instructions in your email as well, Sir," Louis said. "I took the liberty of finding several flight possibilities."

"Thank you, Louis," I said, sincerely grateful. "You have no idea how much this means to me."

"No problem," he said. There was a pause, and then he spoke again. "You're not coming back are you, Mr. Stirling?"

"No." I didn't want it to become public knowledge yet, but I owed Louis at least this much. "Are the Atwoods treating people well?"

"Yes," he answered. "But you are missed, Sir."

"I'm not your boss anymore," I said as I turned on my laptop. "Call me Reed."

"This is good-bye then."

"It is," I said. "If you ever need anything, you call me. Money, a reference, a call to some connection. Anything." I fully intended to send him a nice check for the work he'd done, but I wasn't going to tell him that. He'd argue.

"I'll do that."

I could almost hear the smile.

"Good luck with your young lady, Mr. Stir – Reed."

"Thank you, Louis."

I had a lump in my throat when I ended the call. Louis and I hadn't been close friends, but he'd been one of the few people I'd always been able to count on. I hadn't realized just how much until now. I'd already made my peace with leaving my family, but saying good-bye to Louis somehow made things seem more final.

I pulled up the email he'd sent and opened the attachment. My heart did a strange twist when I saw her. She was dressed formally, but there was no doubt in my mind who she was. "Princess Namisa returns from European vacation." The caption put the picture as having been taken shortly after she'd left me. She had a smile on her face, but even in a picture, I could tell it was forced. I'd smiled like that before, after all. I'd worn it for my engagement announcement. My wedding. Pretty much every public appearance with Britni. I could tell Nami was miserable.

I tore myself away from the picture and scrolled down to the travel information Louis had sent. It seemed there were only three airports in the entire world that flew to Saja and none of them were in the US. The one in Italy had the shortest flight time, but there were also flights out of an airport in India and one in Switzerland. Louis had already made calls and, if I was lucky, I could get on a flight to the Swiss airport today, then fly out of Switzerland and make it to Saja by tomorrow evening.

It wasn't even a question.

I called the airline and made the arrangements as I grabbed something to eat from the kitchen. It was going to be a long flight and airplane food wasn't exactly my favorite thing in the world.

Once I finished, I collected my laptop and went into my bedroom to pack. Two suitcases and a carry-on were all I planned on taking with me, which meant anything I left behind, I wouldn't see again. Fortunately, I'd already figured out which things I wanted and what I could live without, which turned out to be almost everything.

I quickly packed what clothes I could into the

suitcases, then put my laptop in my carry-on with a few other necessities as well as the paperwork I'd done yesterday. Everything was set up, but I wanted to have the papers with me in case some question came up. I'd been serious when I'd said that I wasn't planning on coming back.

I looked at the clock once I'd finished. Twenty minutes before I needed to leave. I could've called my parents or sister, let them know I was leaving, but I had no way of knowing the conversation would end when I needed it to. Better to send off an email right before I got onto the plane. After that, I could turn off my cell phone and not have to worry about returning their calls until I was waiting for my plane in Switzerland.

I picked up my bags and headed out to the town car I'd called. No point in leaving a car at the airport when my ticket was one-way. Plus, I'd already sold mine. As I got into the car, I looked up at the house, expecting to feel a twinge of regret or of sadness. Instead, all I felt was exhilaration. I was going to see Nami and start a new life. The old life fell away and I didn't look back as the town car pulled away from the house. Out with the old and in with the new. No matter what happened from here on out, my life at least would be driven by what I wanted rather than my parents. My life was mine again.

Chapter 9

Reed

I wasn't entirely sure what I'd been expecting when I walked out of the tiny airport, but I was positive it hadn't been this. The sun was on its way down, but the air was still warm for the first week in June. Saja didn't look like Sicily or any of the other European tourist islands I'd been to over the years. It didn't look like Hawaii either, despite the beach I could see from where I stood.

Taxi cabs lined the space in front of the airport and I quickly grabbed one. The driver accepted the Euro I gave him, then shot me a sharp look when I asked him to take me to the palace.

"Why you want to go there?" His English was more heavily accented than Nami's had been, but I could immediately tell they were the same.

I gave him my best charming smile. "I'm an American tourist. We don't have palaces in America."

That seemed to ease his suspicions, but I still got the impression that he wasn't sure how he felt about my request. They didn't seem to have many visitors here, I observed as we drove into the capital. I hesitated to call it a city. I'd grown up in Philadelphia, spent a lot of time in New York and DC for business, traveled to LA, Dallas, Chicago and Miami. Those were cities. This looked more like a town.

Still, it was a nice little place. I saw businesses that had signs in both English and the native language. A couple bookstores and electronics stores. One or two furniture places. Half a dozen clothing stores. I even saw a law firm and a hospital. Granted, they were a fraction of the size of anything in Philly, but it seemed that the little I'd been able to find on Saja had been right. They were fairly self-sufficient.

The car pulled up in front of a pair of massive iron gates. Beyond them, nearly hidden from view by trees, was a massive house that couldn't be anything but the palace. I paid the driver and told him not to wait. It wasn't until I had my suitcases and carry-on on the sidewalk next to me that I realized I hadn't entirely thought this out.

I couldn't exactly walk up to the gate, knock and ask for Nami. Aside from the fact that what I was about to do was most likely against royal protocol, I doubted she'd told her parents anything about me. If I showed up saying that I'd met Nami in Paris, I could get her in trouble, and I still didn't know for certain what that would mean. Saja seemed like a fairly modern place, but when it came to things like the princess's virginity, I wasn't about to take any chances. Not with Nami.

I needed to figure out a way inside without attracting attention. I was at least lucky that I didn't stand out physically from the people of Saja. While the majority of the people seemed to have darker complexions and hair, there had been enough people with fair skin and lighter hair that I didn't stick out like a sore thumb. Passing for a native, or at least a resident, however, wouldn't be enough.

I took my luggage and headed down the sidewalk, circling around the side of the massive fence as soon as it curved away from the sidewalk. The path next to the fence was worn, as if walked often. The fence was overgrown with something that resembled ivy, shielding the view, but it also provided me a place to hide my suitcases and bag.

I felt like an idiot, but I knew I had to see Nami before her parents met me, and that meant I needed to sneak in and find her. I couldn't do that while carrying my things around and I didn't want to waste my time checking into a hotel. It'd be night before I'd be able to make it back here. I couldn't wait that long. The need I'd had for Nami had gotten stronger the closer I'd gotten to her. I had to see her, needed to know that she'd missed me as badly as I'd missed her, that she still wanted me.

I covered my things and looked around to make sure I'd be able to find them again. Satisfied that I'd recognize the hiding spot again, I walked a little further down the path, looking for a place I could sneak in. I had a vague recollection of making fun of the scene in *Romeo and Juliet* where he snuck into the Capulet garden to see Juliet, and smiled to myself. I was probably too old to be making romantic gestures like that, but I was considering this to be more practical than romantic. Or at least that was what I told myself as I found a place where the ivy was thinner, offering me a better look at the grounds.

I was near some sort of service entrance and, as I watched, a smaller gate swung open and a small cart pulled out. I flattened myself against the fence and hoped the ivy would cover me. The cart went the opposite way and I decided to take a chance and quickly slipped through the gate just before it closed behind me.

I could hear people laughing and carrying on inside. The smell of dinner made my stomach growl. I ignored it and moved to the back of the palace. I had absolutely no clue where I was going, a fact that was made abundantly clear when I looked up at the three story building sprawled across several acres. My heart fell. There was no way I'd be able to find Nami before someone spotted me and I got kicked out, or arrested for trespassing.

I could hear Piper's voice in the back of my mind telling me not to give up, but I argued back that she hadn't foreseen this. I'd almost convinced myself to turn around and sneak back out when I heard something. Or rather, someone.

Nami.

"I'm fine, Halea." Her voice was tired, but I knew it. "Go back to your room and get some sleep. You have your English lesson tomorrow."

I followed the sound, arriving in time to see a girl walking out of a door. She was in her teens, with light brown hair, a fair complexion and a petite build. She had only the faintest resemblance to Nami, but I had no doubt this was Nami's sixteen year-old sister, Halea.

I waited until the girl was out of sight before I walked to the door. I didn't want to open it in case there was an alarm, but I wasn't sure knocking was the best idea either. Unfortunately, I had to do one or the other unless I turned around and left.

I knocked.

I heard Nami talking, "Halea, I told you..."

Her voice trailed off as she opened the door and

saw me. Her eyes widened, her face going pale. She recovered quickly, holding a finger to her lips as she shifted so she could partially close the door.

"Gentlemen," she spoke to someone behind her without taking her eyes off me. "My sister and I need to speak in private."

"We're under orders not to leave you."

I recognized Kai's voice.

"I want to talk to my sister without you thugs hovering over me," she snapped. "Run and tell my parents if you want to, but get the hell away from me."

I knew the moment they left because she grabbed the front of my shirt and yanked me towards her, going up on her tiptoes to press her lips against mine. I was so surprised that it took me a moment to respond, but when I did, my arms went around her waist, my mouth opening to let my tongue tease against her lips. She made a sound, crushing her body against mine so that I could feel her full breasts, soft against my chest.

When she finally broke away, she put her hand on my cheek. "What are you doing here?"

"I came for you." I ran my thumb along her bottom lip.

She glanced over her shoulder. "I don't know how long they'll give me, but it should be enough."

I barely had a moment to register the hallway

she pulled me down, but then we were at a door.

"This is the quarters where my personal maid usually stays, but she's not there yet. Walk through the bedroom. There will be a small kitchen and living space. On the other side is another door. It's usually kept locked, but I have the key. It leads into my room." She put her hand on my chest over my heart. "Will you come to me?"

I brushed my lips across hers. "Always."

Her fingers flexed against my chest, and then she turned and hurried away. I opened the door and went inside. It took me a moment for my eyes to adjust, but I was standing in a small alcove. Based on the coat rack, I assumed this was where the maid would've left her shoes and coat before going further into her quarters. I followed Nami's instructions, my body thrumming in anticipation. Waiting until I heard the key turn in the lock was pure torture, but then the door opened and she was there.

I didn't remember closing the door behind me or taking off my shirt, but then her warm hands were on me, fingers tracing over my chest, nails lightly scraping my nipples. I made a sound in the back of my throat as I slid my tongue into her mouth, thoroughly exploring the familiar territory, relearning it.

My hands moved across her back, then down to cup her ass, pulling her tight against me. She moaned into my mouth as she ran her hands around to my back and then down to my ass. I kept one hand on the firm flesh and the other pulled up the back of her shirt, giving my fingers access to her soft skin.

As we tumbled onto the bed, our mouths came apart. Her face was flushed, hair mussed, full lips swollen, and she was the most beautiful thing I'd ever seen. Before I could rid her of her clothes, she pulled her shirt over her head and tossed it to the floor. She wore a strapless bra that barely contained her ample breasts and, as I watched, she reached behind her and undid the clasps, sending the bra to the floor with her shirt.

"My memory didn't do you justice." I cupped her breasts, savoring the weight of them.

I lowered my head to taste her, circling her nipple with my tongue, first one then the other. She buried her fingers in my hair and held me to her breast. Her grip tightened when I took her nipple into my mouth, keeping the suction light at first, then increasing it until she was writhing against me.

When I raised my head, she was breathing heavily, her pupils blow wide with desire. "How quiet do we have to be?" I asked.

She shook her head. "I gave the guards permission to lock me in so they could leave."

I gave her a questioning look. "Why would they

need to lock you in? Aren't they here to protect you?"

She grinned at me, her eyes glinting with that wild streak I'd seen in Venice. "In theory, but lately, it's been more about baby-sitting me. I haven't exactly been the best-behaved princess lately."

My hands went into fists as something occurred to me. Had she been with another man? I looked down at her and saw a shadow on her face as she read my expression. I didn't want to know. After all, I'd been with what's-her-name during the time we'd been apart, and several others. We'd agreed to move on. I couldn't blame her if she'd done the same thing I had.

"It doesn't matter." I kissed her forehead. "As long as you want me now." I looked down at her again, suddenly uncertain.

She kept her eyes locked with mine as she took my hand and slid it under her skirt. Our hands moved between her legs until my fingers were pressed against the crotch of her panties. Her very wet panties.

I took her mouth again, laying her back on the bed as my fingers slipped beneath the crotch of her panties finding her hot and ready. She cried out as I slid a finger inside her and I moaned in response, my cock throbbing at the feel of her pussy clenching around my finger.

I made my way down her throat to her breast, taking her nipple between my lips even as my finger pumped into her, preparing her. I added a second finger as my thumb rubbed back and forth across her clit.

"Please," she begged. "Inside me. Please."

It had been too long. I couldn't wait anymore. I'd go slow later. Right now, I needed to be inside her. I undid my pants even as I pushed her skirt up and climbed between her legs. I shoved my pants down just below my ass, lifting my mouth from her breast so I could see her face as I shoved into her. Her nails dug into my shoulders as her entire body stiffened. I swore, squeezing my eyes closed as she came.

She was still quivering around me when I gathered myself enough to start moving. My thrusts were jerky as I fought my body to put off the inevitable. The pressure inside me was nearly unbearable, the feel of her around me, under me, almost too much.

"Reed."

I opened my eyes when she said my name.

"Let go."

She lifted herself up enough to press her lips against my throat. As I buried myself deep inside her, she bit down on my neck, sending a sharp spike of pain straight through me and pushing me over the edge. I clutched her to me as I came, my body trembling with the force of my orgasm. She wrapped her legs around me, holding me to her, inside her.

It didn't matter that we hadn't seen each other in weeks. It didn't matter that her family had plans for her and that I had no clue what I wanted to do next. Nothing mattered but the fact that we were together, our bodies one. I loved her and that would be enough to overcome any obstacle that came our way. I wouldn't lose her.

Chapter 10

Nami

We made love two more times, and I knew that's what it was, not simply having sex or fucking. No man would've come half-way around the world just for good sex, and especially not a man like Reed. Gorgeous, rich, sweet, charming...he was everything a woman could want, and that wasn't even throwing in how amazing he was in bed. Granted, I didn't have a lot of prior lovers to compare him to, but I had heard people talk enough to know that what I experienced with him wasn't normal. I felt a stab of jealousy at the thought of him being with other women and pushed it aside. I had no right to be jealous. Especially not now.

I could feel him behind me, the heat of his body warming me. I'd left the air conditioning on high through the night and the room was almost chilly. I was glad though because I wanted to enjoy this moment for as long as possible. I'd never thought I'd have this again. I didn't know what it meant for us, for me, but I was trying not to think about it.

"Mmm." He made a sleepy sound, his arms tightening around me. "Good morning."

I opened my eyes, but didn't look up at him. "How did you know I was awake?"

He kissed my temple. "Because the only time you're completely relaxed is when you're sleeping."

How was it he knew that about me? We'd spent all of three nights and one day together. But he was right. I could feel my body tense up the moment I woke. Well, partially right. "Not the only time." I pushed my bare ass back against him and heard him suck in a sharp breath.

He laughed, but there was an edge to the humor. His hand shifted until it was covering my breast. I closed my eyes as desire twisted low in my belly. How could I want him again? My entire body ached from last night, but I didn't care. I just wanted to beg him to take me again. From behind, on top, it didn't matter, so long as he was inside me.

"What time is it?" He kissed the hollow under my ear and I shivered.

I looked at the clock and groaned, but not in pleasure. "It's nearly seven. I need to get up." The last thing I needed was someone bursting into my room to find out why I wasn't awake yet.

"Just a couple more minutes." He squeezed my breast and I felt his cock start to harden against my hip. "We can be quick."

My pussy gave a throb at the thought of it. It would be so easy to say yes, to feel him slide into me. I wondered how different it would feel to have him take me this way. I could imagine his fingers on my clit, bringing me to climax as he spilled inside me...

I sighed. No. It was too risky. Reluctantly, I disentangled myself from his embrace and climbed off the bed. I didn't look at him as I headed into my bathroom. I knew he was smart enough not to leave and risk being seen, so I took my time cleaning up. I needed to think, compose myself.

He'd caught me off guard last night, and once I'd kissed him, that was it. I didn't know what it was about him, but when I touched him, it was like my brain short-circuited. I couldn't think clearly. The fact that I'd brought him into my bedroom when my fiancé and his family were in the guest quarters was proof of that.

Tanek.

Shit.

I pulled on my robe. I definitely couldn't do this naked. It was going to be hard enough with him naked. I had to do it though, no matter how much I hated it. I took a slow breath and let it out, then stepped back into the bedroom.

Reed was sprawled on his stomach, the sheet only half covering his ass. I flushed as I saw the long, red furrows I'd made in his back. He hadn't complained. In fact, if I'd correctly interpreted the sounds he'd been making, he'd liked it.

For a moment, I thought he was sleeping and that I had a bit of a reprieve, but as I walked closer, he rolled over and smiled at me. I didn't smile back. I couldn't. My chest was tight and there was a knot in my stomach that felt like ice. His smile faltered and he sat up, thankfully pulling the sheet across his lap as he did.

"What's wrong?"

I sat on the edge of the bed, but didn't reach for him. "Last night was a mistake."

I felt him tense and his face instantly became a hard mask, unreadable.

"A mistake." His voice was flat.

"I'm engaged, Reed," I said softly. "I told you that my parents would be choosing a husband for me. They have. I have no choice but to marry Tanek."

I stared at her. "You have a choice. There's always a choice."

I could hear the note of desperation in his voice and it hurt my heart.

"I was where you are, and I made the wrong choice," he continued.

"You weren't in the same position," I countered. "This is different. You were worried about letting down your family. I have an entire kingdom to think about."

I stood. He might not have been touching me, but he was still too close. I walked a few steps away and then turned towards him. I couldn't meet his eyes though, and focused on a spot just over his shoulder.

"Just because I don't have a whole country doesn't mean I don't understand responsibility."

I shook my head. I couldn't listen to him. He'd support all of the things I'd been feeling and I'd walk away from my family, my duty...and I'd never forgive myself.

"You're not one of us, Reed." I saw him flinch and forced myself to finish it. "Tanek and I are getting married this weekend. This is my choice. My future is here on Saja with him, not with you."

Chapter 11

Reed

This couldn't be happening. Not after everything I'd done to find her. And I knew it wasn't because she didn't want me the way I wanted her. It wasn't just because we'd slept together again either. I'd seen how she felt, heard it in her voice when she'd called my name. She loved me, I knew it.

But she wasn't choosing me.

Her words hung in the air between us. There was no question about the meaning.

I couldn't look at her as I climbed off the bed and began looking around for my clothes. Something about hearing this while she was clothed and I was naked made it feel all the more humiliating. I winced as I bent down, the skin on my back stretching the marks she'd made. I'd enjoyed it when she'd scratched me, and I'd enjoyed even more the thought that I'd be remembering this encounter for days while we made our plans. Now, the pain made my temper rise.

"You should've told me that when I first showed up," I snapped as I pulled on my pants. "Instead of kissing me and then inviting me back to your room. Making me think there was a chance for us." I grabbed my shirt and pulled it over my head, suppressing a wince as the fabric slid over the scratches. I hoped they'd heal quickly. I didn't want to remember this.

"You're right," she said, her voice infuriatingly calm. "I should have told you then and sent you away."

I turned towards her, bristling at her word choice. "Sent me away? What, like I'm some servant to be dismissed when I've served my purpose?" My hands curled into fists and I fought to keep my voice low. No matter how I felt, I didn't want Nami's bodyguards bursting in to find me here.

Her expression hardened. "Do not presume to understand my thoughts or feelings on the matter."

"Oh, I'm sorry, *Princess*." I spat the last word out as I shoved my feet into my shoes. "Should I be thanking you for letting me fuck you?"

I felt a stab of mingled guilt and satisfaction at the hurt I saw in her eyes.

"Do not speak to me that way." Her posture was stiff, unyielding, her eyes cold.

"Excuse me if I'm a little pissed." I walked around the bed to stand in front of her. Pain overrode my anger for the moment. "Do you have any idea what I gave up to come be with you?"

That was what hurt the most, I thought. She was behaving as if she was the only one who had something to lose here. As if I'd just happened to meander onto her property by happy accident and I could leave now and everything in my life would just go back to normal. No harm done.

"I've been looking for you for over a week. Hired investigators to try to find you because I couldn't stop thinking about you. I liquidated all of my assets, signed over all of my property. I told my family that I was never coming back to the company and left Philadelphia with no plans to return." My voice shook and I paused for a moment to steady it. "I did all of that so when I found you, I would be free to go wherever, be whoever you needed. I gave up everything for you, Nami."

She started to raise her hand like she wanted to touch me, but then dropped it. "I can't."

"Damn you!" I spun around, wanting to hit something. Anything. But I knew it wouldn't be smart. Anything sounding remotely violent would alert whoever was guarding her door. And with the way things were currently going, I'd be lucky if I didn't find myself arrested for rape.

"Reed," she started to speak.

"No!" I turned back towards her, my hands almost shaking with the force of my emotions. "Don't. Don't you dare say my name or make some excuse. It's not that you can't. You won't."

"I have to do what's best for my country." There was a note of pleading in her voice, pleading for me to understand.

I shook my head, refusing to try to see it her way. "No, you're doing what's best for you. What's easy."

"You think this is easy?" Her eyes sparked angrily. "Do you think I wish to be sold off like some prize to the highest bidder? Married to a man whose only interest in me is that I put his child on the throne once I'm gone?"

"I think it's easier to hide behind tradition and duty than it is to follow your heart." I ran my hand through my hair and glanced at the door. We were tempting fate, arguing like this, but I couldn't let her go without a fight. "And I know that your heart is with me." I walked towards her again, this time stopping only when we were mere inches apart. "Tell me I'm wrong."

She looked up at me and, for one terrifying moment, I thought she'd say it. That I was wrong about how she felt about me. That she'd played me this entire time. After what I'd done to Piper, I supposed I would've deserved it.

"It doesn't matter what I think or feel," she said softly. Her eyes slid away from mine.

"Of course it does." I grabbed her chin and held her face in place. "Look at me, dammit!" She did, but her expression was guarded. I forced myself to speak quietly. "What you want matters, and no one who cares about you is going to say otherwise."

She took a step back. "What I want is to marry Tanek on Saturday, as my family desires."

Everything inside me turned to ice.

"Okay, then." I nodded. I couldn't look at her. "If that's what you want."

"I do."

I should've felt pain at those words, knowing she'd be saying them again in only a few days, saying them to bind herself to another man. The man she wanted more than me. The man she'd be with forever. The thoughts piled onto each other until it was hard to breathe, but, still, no pain. I was numb. Every part of me, as if I'd been shot through with Novocain.

"I won't bother you again." The words sounded hollow.

I stepped around her and walked over to the door I'd used the night before. I knew I'd need to be more careful sneaking out than I had been sneaking in, but even the thought of being caught and arrested for trespassing, or whatever else they could throw at me, couldn't spark anything in me. I thought I heard her say my name as I stepped into the maid's chambers, but I didn't stop or turn around. I needed to go, because I knew that once I felt again, it was going to be bad, and I couldn't be here when that happened.

I had enough sense to peek outside rather than just walk out, but everything seemed distant, like I was viewing it from some other place. My brain processed the grounds, the people, but none of it seemed real. I couldn't even feel the door against my fingers as I held it. This entire thing felt like a nightmare, the kind that seemed to go on for years.

I needed to leave. Now. The words prompted no urgency, but I moved anyway. There was a box on the step next to the door. I had no clue what was in it, or if it was important, and I didn't care. I didn't care about anything at the moment. I stepped outside, picked up the box and headed towards the same entrance I had used last night. I didn't know if my attempt at a ruse would work, but it was all I had. Hopefully, everyone would be so busy with wedding preparations that no one would think twice about a stranger carrying a package away from the house.

I passed by a few people who didn't even glance my way and then I was free. I stepped out onto the little side street, dropped the box, and began walking towards where I'd hidden my bags. I didn't know what to do now. Everything I owned was in these two bags. I'd had no plans besides finding Nami. No hotel reservations, no idea of where to go or what to do. I had money and the ability to get even more with a simple phone call and a new bank account.

What good would any of that do me, I thought. I could get a room, but to what end? Saja was beautiful, no doubt, but I had no purpose for being here. No purpose at all, in fact. I was worse off than I'd been when I'd left Philadelphia after Piper.

Piper. I almost laughed. She'd chosen Julien over me and had then told me not to give up on love. Great advice. Love was a joke. It didn't matter, and what was worse, I should've already known this. Duty and honor. Some people respected those. More respected money. Maybe that's what I should do. Find good investments. Make myself even richer than I already was. I'd have women hanging all over me. Gold diggers, but at least I'd know what they were.

I trudged down the sidewalk, ignoring the taxi that passed by. I'd been so sure that when I found Nami, everything would magically fall into place. We'd run away together and plan our future. Whatever she wanted was what I would want.

Only she'd said what she wanted, and it wasn't me.

I felt a faint crack in the numbness. The pain was coming soon and I didn't think anger would be enough to keep it at bay much longer.

Chapter 12

Nami

I heard myself say his name, but there was no conscious thought to it, only my need for him. It was something deep and primal, instinctual. He was in pain and I wanted to go to him, help him, take it away, but I was the cause of that pain. And I had my own to deal with. It was deep and excruciating, like I was tearing apart. The need to go to him only made it worse as I resisted it.

But I had to resist. If I went to him now, I wouldn't be able to give him up, no matter the cost. I'd follow him anywhere, go wherever he wanted. I would leave my family, my home, my responsibilities. The would-be marriage would never happen. My sister would take my place and what would be, would be. Saja would prosper, just as it always had. My parents were young and healthy. They would continue to rule for years. Who knew, maybe, in the future they'd accept my choice and things could be different.

I couldn't risk it though, no matter how much I wanted to. I couldn't take the chance that my parents would try to mold Halea, marry her off as soon as she turned eighteen. It was less than two years away, not enough time for me to convince my parents to change centuries of tradition. And it wouldn't be enough time with Reed. I knew that as soon as I heard the announcement of Halea's engagement, I'd come back. Every moment more I spent with Reed, the harder it would be to leave him if I had to. Better to make a clean break now.

As he walked out of the room and out of my life, I continued to tell myself that I'd done the best thing possible for both of us. Reed needed to forget me, forget that any of this had happened.

Involuntarily, my eyes dropped to the bed. The sheets were still in disarray, the evidence of what we'd done clear. I suddenly needed to be elsewhere. I couldn't stay in this room, the scent of sex and Reed thick in the air. I forced myself not to run. The maids would come in to clean and I couldn't risk any of them figuring out what I'd done.

I went through the motions automatically. Making the bed, straightening things. Lighting a few scented candles. I walked around the room, focusing on the least little thing that might give away my secret. The tension inside me was building, coiling me tighter and tighter until I needed release.

I pulled my robe more securely around my waist and knocked on the door. A moment later, I heard the lock click. Tomas opened the door and stepped aside, letting me out into the hallway. I didn't really want to be in the palace, but if I'd gone out to the grounds the same way Reed had, someone would figure it out and I wouldn't be able to use that particular exit if I really needed it in the future.

I almost laughed as I walked out of the room. I wasn't sure what I thought I'd use it for. Sneak out for another night on the town? I wasn't going anywhere soon. I didn't even get to have a honeymoon like a normal person. The Princess of Saja spent her honeymoon touring the country with her new husband, meeting the people.

The marble was cool beneath my feet and I could hear the footsteps of the guards behind me. Even in my own home, they were there, following. Watching. I wondered how many would come on my honeymoon. I supposed I should be thankful that Saja tradition no longer dictated that there be witnesses for the consummation of the marriage.

I turned down a short hallway and went into the bathroom. I didn't actually need to use it, but it was the only possible way for me to get rid of my bodyguards. I stayed inside for a minute. I didn't know where I wanted to go or what I wanted to do.

Only that I wanted to do it alone.

I slipped out of the other door and cut through the library. I wanted to be outside. There was something about fresh air and sunshine that spoke of freedom more than the richest palace in the world. And freedom was what I craved. Freedom to love and be myself, to make my own choices. I wouldn't ever have that freedom, but I could at least, for a short time, have the illusion of it.

The palace gardens were quite beautiful, perfectly maintained and lush with exotic flowers that were both native to Saja and ones brought in from around the world. My parents often took people into the gardens to impress them. That wasn't where I wanted to go though. What most people didn't know was that there was a small alcove just off of the garden where nature had been allowed to take its course. Wild roses native only to Saja covered the stone walls and the paths were overgrown. I'd often gone there as a child when I wanted to be alone or when I was upset.

Although, I had to admit, my childhood fears and hurts were nothing like what I was feeling right now. I'd never had a broken heart before, not even a childhood crush like most children had. I'd had my fair share of hurts and slights. Even being a princess hadn't kept me from the cruelty of gossip and fake friends. If anything, being who I was had made it worse. But still, nothing could compare to what I was feeling now.

Leaving Reed in Venice had been insanely difficult and it had hurt, but it was nothing like this. I'd been able to tell myself that it had been a simple one-night stand, a crazy fling that I'd get over soon enough. And then he'd come for me. I couldn't brush aside what that had meant. Something had shifted between us.

I didn't know if it had happened when I'd opened the door and saw him or when I'd kissed him, but I did know that by the time I let him into my bedroom, every touch meant more. Neither of us had said anything about it, but I'd known he'd felt it too.

He'd been right. The moment I'd seen him, I should have made him go. Told him about the engagement and sent him on his way. I would've been sad, I knew, but I wouldn't feel like my heart was being ripped from my chest. It was crazy to feel so strongly for someone I barely knew, but I couldn't deny it.

"Princess Nami."

I jumped, stepping off the path and nearly crushing a few bright yellow flowers. I put my hand on my chest, feeling my heart pound against my palm.

"I apologize if I startled you."

Tanek stepped out of the shadow of what I thought was a fruit tree of some kind. The paths through the garden were the same, but the flora had changed since I'd last been here.

"Sorry, I was lost in thought." I managed not to stammer, but it was a close thing. "A lot on my mind."

"I imagine so," he said with a charming smile. "A wedding and a honeymoon are no small feat."

I nodded and stepped back onto the path. I wasn't entirely sure what to say to him. He was going to be my husband and I didn't know how to talk to him. He held out his arm. I didn't want to touch him or have a discussion. All I wanted to do was be alone and cry.

But, I was a princess and princesses rarely got what they wanted, contrary to what most people thought. I smiled at Tanek and hooked my arm through his.

The height difference between us wasn't as much as it was between Reed and I, and I found myself able to look up at Tanek without getting a crick in my neck. I tried studying him objectively, seeing him as I would have if last night, if Venice, hadn't happened. He was handsome, with fairly rugged features. That was good. The people would subconsciously trust him more than they would a 'pretty boy', as the girls in America might say. Even if I was ruler, they would want someone who appeared strong at my side.

"May I ask a question?" Tanek asked, breaking the silence.

"Of course." We went along the curve of the path, away from my private garden. Tanek would share my bed and my life, but I would keep at least one thing for myself.

"Why are you out in the garden in your robe?" His voice was pleasant, but something in me squirmed.

"I woke up and was in the mood for some fresh air." I stopped as the path took us between a small copse of trees. "I missed the gardens while I was away."

"That is right," he said as he released my arm and stepped in front of me. "You attended college in America."

"I did." I resisted the urge to step away, to put some distance between us. I had to get used to it at one time or another, and considering the wedding was in a couple days, it'd probably be a good idea to do it sooner rather than later.

"Did you enjoy your time there?" He reached up to twist a curl around his finger.

When his knuckles brushed against my cheek, it was all I could do not to flinch. His touch was unfamiliar, I told myself. That was all. But Reed's touch had once been the same and I'd reacted differently from that first moment. I'd wanted his hands on my body, his arms, his lips...

I gave myself a mental shake and tried to remember the question. "Yes," I said. "I enjoyed myself."

"I thought so." He took another step towards me, something darkening his eyes. "How much did you enjoy yourself, I wonder?"

My heart thumped painfully against my ribcage. My instincts screamed at me to run, but I was a princess. The future queen of Saja. I did not run from anyone. I squared my shoulders.

"What, exactly, are you implying?" I made my voice as cold as possible.

He put his hand on my waist. "How far did the American boys get?" His hand slid up and grasped my breast.

I jerked back and my palm cracked against his cheek. "How dare you! How dare you speak to me in such a manner, touch me without my permission!" My face was flaming, my temper flaring back to the surface from where it had retreated under hurt. "I am the princess. *Your* ruler."

Tanek's cheek was red, but his eyes were blazing. Before I could react, he grabbed my arm and jerked me towards him. I opened my mouth to scream. I'd have him in jail for this. His fist sank into my stomach, driving the air from my lungs so that all I could do was gasp.

"You are a princess, but you do not rule me." He hissed, his face an inch from mine. "I am to be your husband and you will learn your place."

He shoved his hand between the folds of my robe, groping my breast. His fingers twisted my nipple cruelly, sending pain shooting through me. I cried out, but it wasn't much of a sound.

"Perhaps what you need is to know what it means to be a wife." He released my breast and pushed his hand between my legs.

I fought against him, pressing my thighs together. He let go of my arm and buried his fingers in my hair, yanking my head back. He pulled at the belt of my robe as he dragged me off the path and threw me to the ground.

"How many?" He asked as he pressed his knee into my chest. "How many men did you take, whore?"

I glared at him, hitting at him, for all the good it did. I could barely breathe and my blows were weak. I felt the adrenaline racing through my veins, but it didn't do me any good without oxygen.

"First I shall make you mine." He began to unbuckle his pants. "Then I will punish you for allowing someone else to take what is mine." He wrapped his hand around my throat and leaned down so that his lips were next to my ear. As the world began to go gray, he whispered, "I will be your king and you will obey me."

As he shoved my legs apart, I prayed that the darkness would come and keep me.

Chapter 13

Reed

The capital of Saja, it turned out, had several nice hotels in varying price ranges, all located within walking distance of one of their beautiful beaches. It was the kind of place people would visit and call paradise. The kind of place men would take their wives on their honeymoon, on special anniversaries.

I snorted a laugh and turned away from the window. I'd gotten the best room at the best hotel, almost out of habit rather than any real desire to have a nice room. I hardly noticed it, processing main room, kitchenette, bathroom, bedroom. No details. No appreciation for anything around me.

I walked into the bathroom, stripping as I went. I was exhausted physically, emotionally and mentally. Between the jet lag and the lack of sleep last night, I would've been half-dead on my feet even if I hadn't been through hell emotionally. I stood under the shower spray, barely registering if the water was hot or cold. I was still wrapped in that numb cocoon, but I knew it was like an eggshell, fragile and ready to break at any moment.

I toweled off, dropping it at the foot of the bed before I climbed under the covers. I didn't care that it was still morning, I just wanted to sleep. I supposed I should've been thankful for the jet lag and lack of sleep since I was too tired to overthink anything, then I sank down towards the darkness. For a moment, I saw a flash of Nami's face, of her eyes, and had a sudden, sharp fear that vanished as I fell asleep.

I woke up hours later, with no idea of how much time had passed, only the strange disorienting feeling that came with sleeping during the day. I rolled over and squinted at the clock. Four o'clock. I was never going to get back on the right schedule if I didn't get up now. I could still manage to get to sleep tonight, even if it wasn't until late.

I sat up, rubbing my eyes. My stomach growled and I remembered that I hadn't really eaten much of anything over the past two days. I wasn't hungry in the sense that I wanted to eat, but I knew I needed to. I didn't want to try to figure things out or try to make any sort of decision when I wasn't thinking clearly.

I picked up the phone and called down for room service. Fortunately, I didn't have to wade through native cuisines as they had plenty of other options. I picked a roast beef sandwich and some random sides because they seemed to be the easiest rather than caring anything about appetizing. It also seemed to be a fairly quick preparation as they knocked less than fifteen minutes later. I was halfway to the door before I realized I was naked and had to stop and grab my towel. I wrapped it around my waist, accepted the cart and settled on the sofa to eat.

I didn't really taste anything, more focused on not thinking than I was on the food. I should be thinking. The thoughts were there, buzzing at the back of my mind like bees, but not the nice little honey bees we were supposed to like. No, these were angry bees, ones that wanted to sting and kill.

I sighed and put down what was left of my sandwich. As much as I didn't want to, I needed to figure out what I was going to do now. I'd spent my time in Philadelphia thinking about getting here, and not much about what came after. I'd assumed Nami and I would figure things out when it came time for that. I'd never even considered what I'd do if she didn't want me. Sure, I'd known that was a possibility, but I'd put it up there with the possibility of my plane crashing on the way here. Something that could happen, but a remote possibility.

The thing was, I really didn't believe she didn't

want me. Granted, she'd told me to leave, but she'd also said this was her duty. That meant she wasn't making the decision based on her feelings for me. I just didn't know what to do with that information.

If only I had more time, I was certain I could convince her that I was the right choice for her. The realization hit me and I swore under my breath. I didn't need to convince her. I needed to convince her parents.

Nami felt that it was her duty to marry who her parents chose because that person would be the best for the country. I'd been thinking all this time that I needed to take Nami away from here, that she needed to escape Saja as much as I had Philadelphia. She loved her country and her family though. She didn't necessarily want to get away from them or not be queen. She could still do that and be with me.

If I could convince her parents to let her have a choice in the matter.

I wasn't exactly some pauper bent on marrying her for her wealth or title. I wasn't royalty or anything like that, but my name did mean something back home. With my liquidated assets, I had plenty of money to bring to the table, enough to prove that my interest wasn't financially motivated. I could tell them that I'd fallen for her before I'd known she was a princess. I'd never reveal that we slept together, but I'd at least be able to tell them that we'd spent time together and that I loved their daughter.

I could also tell them how my parents had forced me into a loveless marriage and how badly that had ended. If her parents truly loved her, they would see that they needed to change their traditions and allow her to choose a husband. And if she chose me, I'd agree to sign whatever they wanted. Hand over my assets. Pledge my loyalty. Renounce my citizenship if it would mean Nami and I could be together. They couldn't fail to see my dedication to Nami if I did all of that.

There was no guarantee it would work. No way of knowing if they'd even care that I loved her. In their minds, doing what was right for the country might be what was right for Nami. Securing her position as future queen, giving her a husband who would have the support and backing of the people. I had to consider that as well. Perhaps they wanted to be able to let Nami choose but knew that if she chose poorly, the people wouldn't follow her.

She'd been right when she'd said that I didn't understand, that I wasn't like her. I didn't know the people of Saja. I'd done as much research as I could while on the plane over here, but there wasn't a lot of information. It was an isolated country with no prominent citizens in any particular field. For all I knew, this isolation caused the people to be suspicious of outsiders. I'd gotten no feelings of animosity, but I appeared to be a tourist. A rich American here to spend money and strengthen their economy. Would they feel different if they knew I wanted to be a member of their royal family? Not to rule them, but simply because I loved one of them. Would love make a difference to them? Just because they were progressive enough to accept a female monarch didn't mean they would allow an outsider in.

There were hundreds of questions, thousands of possibilities, and no way of knowing without trying. Nami had told me to leave, that she was choosing Tanek, but I'd come too far to completely give up without even an attempt.

First thing tomorrow, I told myself. I'd go back to the palace, but not to sneak in this time. I'd ask to see the king and queen. I hoped they'd be intrigued enough at the idea of some random American man wanting to talk to them that they'd overlook the fact that I didn't have an appointment. Once there, I would tell them who I was and what I wanted. If they threw me out, at least I'd know I'd tried.

And what if they agreed? What if they said Nami could choose without losing her birthright? Was I willing to stay in Saja, a king in name while my wife ruled? Yes, I thought, I would do that. I didn't care about the power and I'd already made up my mind that I wasn't going back to Philadelphia anytime soon.

Then there was the alternative. What if her parents allowed her the choice, but she didn't choose me? What if, once she'd met Tanek, she'd fallen for him, realized that what she felt for me was nothing more than the thrill of the forbidden, that she wanted a man of Saja at her side, someone who understood her world. I wasn't sure my heart could take another blow like that, especially not with Nami. I'd run to Europe to escape the pain when Piper had chosen Julien over me. Where could I go if it happened again? Where else could I run?

I had a sudden and laughable flash of me in Australia with surfers and kangaroos. I didn't laugh though. Nothing about this was funny.

Time crept by, each agonizing second worse than the last. I was torn between elation at my plan and the certainty of success, and depression at the thought that it would fail miserably, that I'd end up adrift again, no future, no plans, no hope. Logically, I knew it was foolish to put all of my hopes and dreams into a woman, but this wasn't exactly a normal situation. Everything hinged on what happened tomorrow.

I'd always loved the Robert Frost poem about the two roads and taking the one less traveled, mostly because I'd never done that myself. I could honestly say that, until I'd met Piper, I'd never actually felt like I was at that fork. I'd screwed things up with her, no matter how I ended up feeling about her, but I wasn't going to do that now. I didn't know what would happen tomorrow, but I knew that, no matter what, I'd be on one of two paths that I'd never even considered before.

I stayed up until midnight before heading to bed again. This time, my busy brain was louder than my need for sleep and I spent hours tossing and turning. Some of it was the time difference, but enough was my inability to turn off my thoughts. It was well into the early morning hours before I finally fell asleep. I woke a few hours later, still tired, but at least coherent enough to think straight.

I showered and shaved, scraping off two days' worth of stubble, and then went about the task of figuring out what to wear. I had a suit and a tux in my bags, but I wasn't sure if I wanted to appear in either one. I didn't know enough about Saja practices and customs to know if too formal was bad. Would they see the suit as me trying to impress them? It was an expensive one. Or, would they take it as a sign that I respected them, understanding their position? The tux was definitely too much.

In the end, I decided that a suit and a humble attitude would be the best possible combination. I'd show her family that I had money, but that I didn't care about it. Some guys couldn't pull that off, generally because they were lying, but since I really didn't care about money, I could do it. It was a fine line to walk. That was good though. It gave me something to concentrate on besides worrying about what could happen. And that, at least, I had some control over.

By mid-morning, I was ready to go. Well, at least physically. I was dressed and looked like my old self, the CEO who'd been managing his family's company for years. The son of a prominent Philadelphia family. I wasn't conceited, but I knew that I was considered quite the catch back home, and if my time in Europe was any indication, I wasn't exactly considered unappealing outside of the States either. But I wasn't trying to impress Nami. I needed to impress her parents, and I had a feeling that my normal charming self might not be up to the task.

I pushed aside the negative thought and headed down to the front of the hotel to catch a cab. There weren't very many cabs on the island, but it was easy enough to find one here. I got the same strange look as before when I asked to be taken to the palace, but he didn't pry, which was good because I didn't have any idea what I'd say.

When I got out at the gates, my heart was hammering and my mouth was dry. This was it. I could either get back in the cab and give up or I could do what I came to do. I took a breath as the cab drove off. I didn't really have a strategy here, so I figured the most obvious thing was my best bet. I walked up to the gate and hit the buzzer.

A minute later, a heavily muscled guy with what looked like a very big gun on his belt approached. He wasn't smiling, but he also wasn't pointing the gun, so I took that as a good sign.

"Hello." I was tempted to put my hands in my pockets but I didn't want him thinking I was reaching for something. I had to approach this place like I was walking up to the White House.

"American?" The guard seemed mildly amused, which I supposed was better than angry or wary.

I nodded and grinned. "My name's Reed Stirling and I'm from Philadelphia. I'd like to speak with the king and queen."

His eyes widened and, for a moment, I thought he was going to call the cops. Instead, he laughed. "And for what reason should I tell them you are here?"

Shit. I hadn't thought about that. I couldn't exactly tell this guy that I was in love with Nami. He'd either call someone to lock me up because I was crazy or think I was a threat. Besides, I had a feeling that wasn't something her family would want getting out, even if they did end up accepting me. I'd definitely have to be part of some big PR thing. I could, however, tell a partial truth.

"I met their daughter." I almost called her Nami and then remembered that wouldn't be how she was known here. "Princess Namisa. While she was in Paris. Saja sounded wonderful, so I came to visit, and I'd like to pay my respects."

He looked skeptical, but he didn't tell me to leave. He picked up his radio and said something in his native language. After a minute, someone answered back and the guard came over to the gate and punched in a code. The gate slid open and I stepped through. I stopped, letting the guard pat me down.

"The king and queen will see you in the receiving room."

Chapter 14

Reed

My first thought as I walked into the receiving room was that I was glad they hadn't taken me to their throne room – if they had one. This room was intimidating enough. I was rich and I'd seen the best of Philadelphia's best, but I was impressed. Expensive furnishings, beautiful artwork. I didn't even see the people for several seconds.

A pair that I felt confident assuming were the king and queen sat directly across from the door. They weren't on thrones, but I was willing to bet the chairs were at least a couple hundred thousand dollars. Their clothes were even more expensive than mine.

"May I present Mr. Reed Stirling of Philadelphia, Pennsylvania?" A man I couldn't see announced me and I stepped further into the room.

And that's when I saw her.

Nami was sitting at her father's other side, back straight, face carefully expressionless. A man sat next to her. He had black hair, ice blue eyes and an arrogant look that made me want to hit him. Then I saw his hand clasp Nami's possessively and my fingers curls into fists. If I hadn't suspected who he was before, I knew it now.

Tanek.

Nami's fucking fiancé.

I'd not really thought of him at all except in the vague idea of the engagement, but now I realized I hated him. Marrying Nami might not have been his choice any more than he was truly hers, but the way he was holding her hand said that he was staking his claim. He didn't know who I was, I was sure of it, but he was making sure I knew what his position here was.

"Mr. Stirling, I present King Amir, Queen Persephone, their daughter Princess Namisa and her betrothed, Tanek Nekane," the same man spoke again.

I gave a bit of a bow, feeling awkward as I did it, but based on the expression on the king and queen's faces, it had been the right thing to do.

"We do not find many Americans willing to make the appropriate gestures to royalty," King Amir spoke.

I gave a smile and a slight nod. I wasn't sure if

they were the kind of monarchs who'd take offense with someone looking at them directly, but I figured I'd risk it. I wanted to see what I could of them, see what of Nami I could find. The physical part was easy. She looked like both of them. The personality was harder. I wondered from which she'd gotten her stubborn streak.

"You mentioned you met our daughter in Paris?" Queen Persephone spoke. Her tone was polite, but empty. She would've done well in business...and poker.

"I did." I risked a glance at Nami now, expecting to see her worried that I would give her away. She didn't look concerned though, or at least from what I could see. She wouldn't meet my gaze.

"And may I inquire just how that occurred?" King Amir asked.

I was on dangerous ground here, and I knew it. Anything I said to her parents could possibly hurt her, but with Tanek sitting right there, it could do even more damage. I opened my mouth to give them some sort of lie about how I'd met Nami, but I didn't get a chance.

"Mr. Stirling was on the train with me," Nami said. "From Paris to Venice. When the train was delayed, the two of us talked to pass the time."

The smile on my face felt fake, but I knew it looked fine. I'd had a lot of practice at home. I nodded as if in agreement. I would've preferred to keep it as close to the truth as possible, but she knew her parents. If this was the best transition into my declaration, then I'd go along with it. I just wished Nami's fucking fiancé would stop staring at me. I was nervous enough about proclaiming my feelings without him giving me the evil eye. I'd hoped to talk to the king and queen only, to convince them and then surprise Nami. But, if this was my only choice, I would do what needed to be done.

"Mr. Stirling is the head of his family's business in America," Nami continued. Her tone was pleasant, but there was no warmth in it. Nothing to let me know what she was thinking. "I believe he mentioned something about coming to Saja to determine if he might find business opportunities here."

"So you have come to introduce yourself and present us with a business proposal?" King Amir asked.

I kept my eyes on Nami for a few seconds longer, willing her to look at me, to show me what she was feeling. Was she saying this because she knew my real reason for being here and didn't want me to do it? Who was she more worried about me speaking to, her parents or her fiancé? Or did she think I'd tell too much?

I looked back at the king and queen. "I don't

have a business proposal ready, your Majesties. I simply wished to meet you and establish an acquaintance in the hopes that we may someday have a working relationship."

I chose each work carefully. When Nami and I told them the truth, at least about what we meant to each other, my words could be interpreted different ways so they wouldn't think I'd been completely dishonest.

"That is quite enterprising of you."

I couldn't tell if Nami's father was impressed or being sarcastic in that subtle, annoying way that only members of high society – and apparently, nobility – could manage.

"Thank you," I said, giving a bland smile that he could either take as genuine or as me letting him know that I knew how he meant it.

"Now, Mr. Stirling, if you will please excuse us." Queen Persephone stood. "As a visitor, I am sure you have not heard, but Princess Namisa will be married on Saturday, and we have much planning to do."

"Of course." I resisted the urge to look at Nami again. The way the queen was looking at me made me think it was possible she suspected there was more to the story than we were saying. I didn't think that was a good thing, particularly based on what she'd just said. Nami's expression hadn't changed, and she still wasn't looking at me.

"Tomas and Kai will show you out," King Amir said.

Fuck.

The pair came towards me, their faces blank, but their eyes clearly said that if they had their way, they'd be throwing me rather than showing me, and making sure I had a few 'accidents' along the way. I smiled towards the king and queen one last time before turning around to allow myself to be escorted from the room. It took everything I had not to look at Nami again, but I could feel the tension radiating off of the two bodyguards and knew they were looking for any excuse to teach me a lesson.

We walked down the hallway towards the front doors, the guards half a step behind me so they could react if I tried to move. I wasn't dumb enough to run. Nami's parents would never accept me if I disrespected them in such a manner. I did need to see her though, talk to her alone. I needed her to know that I was willing to fight for her if she'd let me.

As we reached the front of the palace, another man opened the door, his face professionally blank. I stepped through the door, stopping as Kai grabbed my arm. His voice was low in my ear, but the volume didn't detract from the sincerity or the menace in his words.

"Stay away from the princess. If I see you again, I will present your balls to the king."

I didn't make any indication of acknowledgement, but he didn't seem to need one. He released my arm with a bit of a shove and I walked down the stairs. The front gates opened and I walked through them, turning the corner so that I was hidden from sight. I needed to figure out what I was going to do. I hadn't been able to complete my plan, so I didn't know where to go next.

I wasn't sure if it was smart to try for the other entrance again, so I began to walk in the opposite direction, hoping I'd be able to spot some way in. The security I'd seen had been good, but not fool-proof. It was clear that, while the royal family warranted protection, they weren't expecting some sort of attack. From what I'd read about Saja, it made sense. They were a peaceful country. Barely any crime at all, and only a small portion of it violent. Most of those were mild, like fist fights over stupid things, often while drunk. Saja had only one prison, and it had never been filled to capacity. In a country like this, excessive security would've been perceived as either a barrier between the people and their sovereign, or as a show of mistrust.

I fully planned to take advantage of that.

As I rounded the corner and headed along a quiet side street, I spotted something several yards ahead. A gate, barely big enough for one person to fit through, was opening. Covered with plants, I never would've known it was there, and based on how loudly it squeaked, it wasn't a commonly used entrance.

I wasn't sure if I should hide or hurry towards it and I stopped, caught in indecision. Then I saw a familiar figure step out onto the sidewalk.

"Nami." I breathed a sigh of relief and jogged towards her.

As I grew closer, I saw more than I had in the throne room. Her expression wasn't just impassive, but rather guarded, like there was something she didn't want me to see. Something else seemed off too, but I couldn't figure out what it was. She looked different, as if in the short time since I'd last seen her, something had changed.

"Why did you come, Reed?" Her voice was soft and she fixed her gaze at a point over my shoulder.

I reached for her hands, but she didn't respond, her fingers staying limp and cold in my hands. "I came for you. I want us to be together. I know you don't think it's possible, but I think I could convince your parents to give me a chance."

Now she did look at me, a moment of surprise flitting across her eyes before they went blank again. "Give you a chance?"

I nodded, sliding my hands up her arms until I

was grasping her shoulders. "I'm not nobility, or from Saja, but I'm not from some poor, backward family. We're well-respected in Philadelphia." I didn't bother to add that our position in society was in a bit of peril at the moment. It wouldn't help things and I had no idea how long that trouble would even last. Rich people were easily distracted even if they never truly forgot.

She started to shake her head, but I kept going before she could protest.

"I have money so it's clear I'm not after that. I know how to behave around high society so I wouldn't embarrass you. I'd sign any sort of paperwork they asked. Renounce my citizenship and become a naturalized citizen of Saja. Whatever it would take to show your parents that I'm serious."

Her voice was soft. "It's too late."

My smile faltered. "No," I said. "I refuse to accept that."

"Contracts have been signed." She lifted her chin, but didn't meet my gaze. "The wedding on Saturday is a mere formality. For all intents and purposes, Tanek is my husband."

"No," I repeated, my tone harder in disbelief and denial.

I closed the distance between us, reaching out to cup the back of her head as I lowered my mouth to hers. Her lips parted with a gasp of surprise and I slid my tongue between them. For a brief, wonderful moment, her body relaxed into mine, her mouth pliant as my tongue explored. She was mine.

Then her hands were on my chest, pushing rather than pulling. The kiss broke, leaving me gasping, my body aching. I stepped back, hands clenched at my sides. I wanted her so badly, but her actions had said to stop, and I did.

"What's done is done, Reed." She folded her arms across her middle as if hugging herself. "Go home. There's nothing for you here."

She stepped back through the hidden gate and I heard it latch behind her. I stayed there for a long time, but she didn't return. It was over.

Chapter 15

Nami

The white silk whispered against my legs as I followed him into the bedroom. It had been a beautiful wedding, the kind most girls would dream of. Flowers had been everywhere, each one chosen specifically for the occasion. Their scents had been perfectly blended so that the effect wasn't overwhelming. The palace ballroom had been decorated in sprays of white and gold, every inch of the place cleaned so that it had shone. The gold bridesmaid's dresses had been simple, elegantly cut for each bridesmaid to flatter the different figures. After all, a royal wedding wasn't about the bride.

Through it all, however, I hadn't been able to stop thinking about the wedding night. Ancient traditions would have stated that at least one of my parents, or a selected member of nobility be in the room as the marriage was consummated, but, fortunately, that practice had been discontinued generations ago. My father's great-grandfather had been the last to follow that particularly embarrassing scenario.

Tradition did still, however, require my parents, the wedding party and certain select guests, to escort us to the bridal suite. Last night had been my final night in my childhood bedroom. Those quarters were now being emptied and cleaned in preparation for a nursery. My new quarters would be with my husband.

As the doors shut behind us, I didn't even see the beauty of our room, the candles that had been lit to offer us dim, romantic lighting. All I saw was him. He turned towards me and I realized my hands were shaking.

It was silly of me to be nervous. This wasn't my first time, or even our first time. I already knew his body, knew the pleasure it could give me. But this wasn't like other times. We were married. When we came together tonight, it would be not only with my parents' blessing, but with that of the entire country. He would be my king, the father to my children.

He came towards me, his dark eyes nearly black in the dim light. He reached out and carefully removed each of the decorative pins that had kept my wayward curls manageable. With each one, he let his fingers graze my skin, sending a blaze of heat through me. By the time he was finished, the shaking in my hands came from an entirely new place.

I pushed his jacket from his shoulders, letting it fall to the floor as I moved on to his shirt. The desire inside me grew with every inch of skin revealed. He was so beautiful, his body a work of art.

It wasn't until both of us were naked that he finally kissed me, one hand buried in my hair, the other at the small of my back. I pressed my body against his as our tongues twined together, my nipples hardening with the friction. His cock was half-hard against my stomach and I could feel it swelling even as my own body responded.

I dimly wondered if it would always be like this, if I would always want him so badly that it hurt. It wasn't just the physical desire, the aching to be filled. It was him and being close to him. Our bodies joined, souls coming together. I'd always considered myself a complete person before, but with him, I knew I'd been only half of myself.

He laid me on the bed and propped himself up on one elbow to give his free hand the chance to explore. He started at my face, his fingers tracing each eyebrow, then down to my cheekbones. When he ran his finger along my lips, I parted them, darting out my tongue to touch his skin.

"Do you have any idea how beautiful you are?"

*he asked as his hand continued its journey, sliding
down my throat, then across my collarbone, before
dancing between my breasts.*

*I reached up and pushed back his golden hair.
"You're beautiful," I said sincerely.*

*He smiled, a full smile that made his entire face
light up. He caught my hand, holding it in place as
he turned his head and kissed my palm. When he
released my hand, he lowered his head to my
breasts, placing light kisses across the skin. My eyes
wanted to close, but I kept them open, wanting to
watch him take my nipple between his lips.*

*I gasped at the heat of his mouth, then swore as
he began to suck on the overly sensitive flesh. His
hand caressed my thigh, adding to the heat already
pooling in my belly. My back arched, wanting
more. When he raised his head, I made a sound of
protest.*

*"Shh, baby." He shifted his hand to my stomach,
his thumb making small circles on my skin. "We
don't have to rush. No one's going to stop us." He
kissed my neck, my jaw, my lips.*

*He was right, I knew. We were married. The
matching platinum bands on our fingers said that
we were going to be together forever. We weren't
going to be interrupted by Tomas and Kai. There
would be no panic over whether or not we should
be doing this. No rush to hurry because we had*

limited time. It wasn't just that it was no longer wrong, but rather that it was expected.

I was pulled out of my thoughts by the feeling of Reed's hand sliding around to my inner thigh. My eyelids fluttered as his tongue slowly circled my breast, moving up my golden skin to my nipple. As his fingertip ghosted over my lower lips, I finally let my eyes close.

The sensations surrounded me, overwhelmed me. There was the scent of him, spicy and masculine. Something so uniquely him that I would know it anywhere. The feel of him. His skin. The shape of his hands, his mouth. The heat from his body and mouth.

I moaned as his teeth scraped my nipple. How did he know that I needed those little pinpricks of pain? That my body craved an intensity that gentle caresses couldn't give me.

A finger circled my entrance and I squirmed. He chuckled, the vibration moving down through my breast even as he slid his finger inside.

I moaned, but I needed more. My eyes opened and I reached over to clutch at Reed's shoulders.

"Please." The word became a cry as a second finger joined the first. He curled them and my entire body went stiff.

Even while I was still in the midst of orgasm, I felt him shove his way inside me, stretching me, *opening me. I wanted to scream, but it was as if all the air had been pushed from my lungs. The intensity of what I was feeling, physically, emotionally, it was almost too much.*

Our bodies rocked against each other, friction and heat. My nails raked his back and his teeth worked over my skin. My world was narrowed down to our two bodies and where they were joined. He was mine and I was his, our hearts, minds and bodies made one. The rings didn't make it so. We'd been this way from the first moment we'd come together.

"Mine," I whispered possessively in his ear.

"Yes," he said. "Yours. And you are mine."

"I am," I agreed. I could feel another climax building. "Forever."

My muscles began to tremble...

I jerked awake, my body flushed and shaking with the force of the dream. I'd woken just before coming, leaving me bereft and tense. For a moment, I thought that was what had woken me, my body not able to take a second orgasm and still stay asleep. Then I realized that wasn't it at all.

Someone was in my room.

My heart leaped into my throat as I saw the shadowed figure sitting on the edge of my bed. Reed had come back. He'd known how I felt, the feelings I'd refused to name or think about, and had come to me.

The light next to the bed suddenly switched on and I swallowed a scream.

"Tanek." My voice came out more breathless than I wished it would have. I grabbed my blanket, pulling it up to my neck. I saw something flicker in his eyes and knew it had been the wrong move.

"You seemed to be enjoying your dream," he said.

"You should not be in here." I straightened, trying to regain my composure. My heart was pounding, the adrenaline racing through my system making me hyperaware of everything.

I'd scrubbed my skin nearly raw, but I could still feel every place he'd touched me. I hadn't wanted to look in the mirror this morning, but I'd forced myself, knowing I'd need to make sure I chose clothes that would cover the bruises. Tanek had either been lucky or he'd known what he was doing. He hadn't made a mark on my face and the ones on my neck were faint enough to be covered with make-up. The rest of me was another story.

I resisted the urge to pull my legs up. Aside from the fact that I didn't want Tanek to see another gesture made in response to him, I also knew it'd hurt enough to show on my face. He hadn't been satisfied to take me only once. I refused to think about the things he'd done to me, not knowing if I'd be able to maintain my composure if I remembered.

"I do not believe you should be telling me what I should or should not be doing." Tanek's voice was low and threatening. "On Saturday, I will be your husband and I will do as I please."

My temper began to rise, pushing through the fear and the hurt. Who the hell did he think he was? I'd agreed to marry my parents' choice because it was the right thing to do for Saja. I hadn't said anything to them today about what had happened, because I was still trying to figure out the best way to do it. Just going to the hospital and reporting an assault wasn't exactly an option for me.

"Get out of my room." I spoke through gritted teeth. "And I want you out of my home."

I expected anger, violence, outright refusal. What I didn't expect was laughter. A sharp, sardonic chuckle that managed to both piss me off and frighten me.

"I will leave your room...when I am ready." He reached over and grabbed my wrist, squeezing until I winced. "And I will not be leaving this house. MY house. I will be king and Saja will be mine."

He leaned closer and I could smell the alcohol on his breath. He wasn't drunk, but he wasn't entirely sober either.

"I will tell my parents what you did," I threatened.

"No," he said. "You will not, or I will tell them you were not a virgin when I took you."

My eyes narrowed. "They will not believe you."

"Don't be so sure about that," he said, his eyes cold. "But it doesn't matter. You will never say a word about what happened to anyone. Remember, accidents happens. It wouldn't surprise me if suddenly an accident happened that would leave me free to wed another. A real virgin."

I felt like I'd been punched in the stomach. He wouldn't.

"Your sister, Halea, is a virgin, I am certain. For now." He smiled. "I will spend the next two years teaching her how to please me, and then I will marry her. She will be queen in name until she gives me a son, and then she will join you."

"Keep your fucking hands off of my sister!" I put as much venom into my voice as I could, but the words fell flat.

A sharp pain shot through me as I felt his strong fingers dig deep into the skin of my arm. He hissed in my face. "Then you better do everything I fucking ask of you. Pretend all you must, but you *will* obey me, bare my children...my son, our future king. It's you or Halea. Your choice."

He would do it, I knew. He would kill me, rape Halea, force her to marry him and most likely kill her too. I'd seen it in his eyes. He was capable of anything.

Before, I'd chosen to marry him to protect Halea from our parents forcing her onto the throne. Now, I knew I had to choose Tanek to save not only my life, but my sister's.

Chapter 16

Reed

I should've left Saja right after Nami had rejected me...again. The entire island was buzzing about the wedding. Even staying in my hotel room didn't keep me safe. The staff was cheery and constantly asking if I'd heard the wonderful news. Looking out the window was just as bad. The entire capitol was getting ready. There were flowers and streamers and all sorts of other things I might've found interesting if they hadn't meant the woman I loved was about to marry someone else.

Maybe that was why I'd stayed. To punish myself for what I'd done. For what I'd failed to do.

I ran my hand through my hair. I'd spent Friday pacing and trying to avoid the view while smiling politely at the people who brought my room service. I hadn't slept at all Thursday night, and last night hadn't been much better. Now, it was just after dawn and I didn't know what to do.

There would've been flights yesterday. Not many since it wasn't a big airport, but enough to get me out, especially if I hadn't cared where I was going. But I hadn't gone yesterday. Even though today was a Saturday and most airports ran on Saturday, today was a holiday of sorts. Nothing was open. Even the hotel had informed me that, during the wedding, no services would be available.

The palace was huge, but not big enough to support all of Saja's citizens, so the whole thing would be broadcast on Saja's only local station.

I wasn't planning on watching it. Or, at least, not on TV. I'd had a very bad idea that had woken me before the sun had come up, and I was currently arguing with myself about it.

I should go home. Back to Philly with my tail between my legs. My parents would be more than happy to let me take over again, no matter how I'd left things. The last time I'd seen Piper and Julien, it had been a bit awkward, but I'd gotten the impression that they wouldn't have been against a real friendship. And no matter what Piper had told me, I knew she'd understand why I'd given up. I could pursue Nami to the ends of the earth, but if she didn't want me, there wasn't anything I could do about it.

The thing was, I still didn't entirely believe that she honestly wanted Tanek. Something had happened after I left her. Something had changed that had made her choose to not believe in me. I didn't know what it was, but a part of me still didn't believe it. And I was pretty sure I wasn't going to believe it until I saw that ring on her finger...maybe not even then.

That was why I had to go. I couldn't just sit in my room and watch it on television. I had to actually be present, in the room, hear her say her vows. I needed to know that she was going to follow through, that she had gotten the life she wanted. I had to see that she didn't hesitate during any part of the ceremony, see that she meant what she said.

It would be painful. Awful. One of the worst things in the world to watch, especially if she went through with it. It would take all of my willpower to stay silent if they went with the traditional question about anyone speaking up if they knew why a couple shouldn't be married. I was also pretty sure that I'd get in some serious trouble if any of the royal family, the bodyguards or the fucking fiancé saw me.

But I had to go.

I knew it deep down in my gut, and I'd known it all day yesterday. If she was going to stop the wedding, I had to be there to stand with her when she did it. If she went through with it, I had to be there to see it happen so I could move on. I still wasn't entirely sure how I would manage to do that, but I figured I should probably take things one step at a time. After all, I was about to do something so stupid it could land me in Saja's only jail if I was caught.

My plan was pretty simple. I already knew where the service entrance was and I also knew rich people. They didn't really look at the help. I didn't have anything that could let me pass for kitchen staff or something like that, but I did have a tux that I could wear and pretend to be one of the staff hired for inside the house. Most of the time, it wasn't about the clothes anyway. It was the attitude.

A couple hours later and I was standing inside the ballroom of the Saja palace. I'd gone through the open service gate with a huge vase of flowers, then spent the rest of the time before the wedding letting myself be ordered around by some high-strung woman in a serious-looking peach business suit. I'd waited until the last possible minute and managed to slip into the back of the room. Huge statues stood around the edges of the room and I tucked myself into the shadows. I knew I'd be practically invisible now, and that was what I wanted.

The bridesmaids came first. I recognized the girl I'd seen that night, the one I knew had to be Halea. The girl Nami was sacrificing her own happiness for. I had to admit, when I looked at that sweet, innocent face, I couldn't blame her. I didn't even know the girl and I wanted to protect her.

I turned with the rest of the crowd to watch as Nami walked in. Her dress was simple and elegant. White silk fitted to complement not only her coloring, but her figure as well. There was no veil or elaborate train, and the dress itself was relatively unadorned. I wasn't really paying much attention to the dress, however. I was too busy watching her face.

She was staring straight ahead, eyes fixed on her destination. While she was smiling, I could tell it was fake. She didn't look at her fiancé the entire way and, as I glanced towards Tanek, I saw that he wasn't looking at Nami either. He might've been turned in that general direction, but he wasn't watching her.

I didn't understand how they could do this. It was clear that neither one of them loved the other. Hell, they barely knew each other. How could Nami agree to marry this guy? Him, I got. Nami was rich and would be the queen someday. By marrying her, he'd be king and his kids would get to rule Saja one day. And if what Nami had said was true, he could fool around as much as he wanted because his bastards wouldn't have a claim on the throne. Nami's line was the one that mattered. So long as he got her pregnant, it wouldn't matter who else he knocked up.

My hands clenched at my sides. I didn't want to

think about Nami conceiving a child with him, with anyone besides me. The realization hit me hard enough that I physically felt it. It wasn't that I just didn't want her to sleep with him. Yes, I hated the thought of him touching her, kissing her, being inside her, but it was more than that. I could picture her in my mind's eye, her stomach swollen with a child, and I knew that I wanted it to be my child.

I'd never really thought about kids before, not in any real sense. With Britni, we'd been expected to have a child, but I'd never imagined it, and certainly had never pictured Britni pregnant. I'd always wanted kids, but the idea had been far off, in a distant future, no matter how the years had passed. I hadn't even thought about them with Piper. Even though I'd insisted that I was in love with her, I'd never once imagined a future beyond a wedding. I hadn't considered what it would be like to grow old with her, what kind of mother she would've been. I knew she'd be a good one and when I thought of her and Julien having a child, I liked the picture I saw in my head.

I didn't want just a few more days or months with Nami. I wanted forever and everything that came with it. I wanted the strange food cravings and being yelled at in the delivery room. I wanted late night feedings and irritability from lack of sleep. I wanted the terrible two's and teenage rebellion. I wanted all of that as long as she was at my side. Dark curls streaked with silver. Aching bones and fading eyesight. All of the things that came with old age, they didn't scare me when I thought of going through them with her.

Her voice drew me back to the present. She was reciting her vows, repeating words similar to the ones I'd said not too long ago. I supposed it was hypocritical of me to question her choice, or to assume that her fiancé was only after the power and money. Hadn't I been there, marrying a woman I didn't love because it was what my parents expected of me? How could I fault either of them when I'd made the same choice? I would have regretted it now if it hadn't been for the fact that, had I not married Britni, Piper never would have chosen Julien and I wouldn't have left Philadelphia in the first place, which meant I never would've met Nami.

I had sometimes wondered if I hadn't married Britni, if Piper and I would have lasted. I knew we would've at least been together for a while because we'd had a true physical attraction to each other and had enjoyed spending time together. What I didn't know was if it would've led to a life in happiness or if she would've come to the same conclusion, that we really didn't love each other, not in the way we needed to.

As Nami and her fiancé joined hands, my heart

twisted. It was almost over and Nami hadn't stopped it.

Had it been this way for Piper, I wondered. Had she felt sick to her stomach? Like her heart was being ripped from her chest? Like she couldn't get enough air into her lungs? I'd thought a lot about my wedding day over the short time Britni and I had been married. I'd thought about what would've happened if I'd stopped the ceremony, told Britni that I couldn't do it. If I'd walked down the aisle and claimed Piper right then. I'd never once tried to imagine what she must've been going through during the ceremony.

Was there a difference though? She'd said herself that we weren't truly in love. What I felt for Nami was real. I knew it in every fiber of my being, every cell. I'd never believed in soulmates or true love, even with Piper. Nami made me question everything I'd ever known. I wasn't whole without her. She was the one. The only one.

I missed the pronouncement, but looked up just in time to see Tanek kiss her. It was a fairly chaste kiss, but I could see the possessiveness even from where I stood. Tanek was making it clear to everyone present that Nami was his.

I leaned against the wall as the couple were presented to their people. I no longer trusted my legs to hold me. The pair walked down the aisle,

Nami's arm looped through Tanek's, their stride evenly matched, as if they moved in perfect sync. Neither of them looked at anyone in the crowd and I was glad. I didn't want Nami to see me, and more than that, I didn't want to see her face, meet her eyes. I didn't think I could bear it if I saw her look at me with pity.

The wedding was over and the reception would begin shortly, so I knew I needed to leave. I forced my legs under me and began to walk out the way I'd come. I wasn't nearly as careful, but I wasn't seen. I wouldn't have cared if I had been spotted. Nothing mattered anymore. It was over.

Chapter 17

Nami

I wasn't entirely sure what I was expecting from my wedding day, but I did know that, as a child, when I'd pictured getting married, I'd always thought I would at least be happy. I'd always known that I wouldn't be allowed to choose my spouse, but when I was young, I'd dreamed that the man my parents chose would still, somehow, be the man of my dreams. He'd be worthy of the title prince, and later, king. A fairy tale in which the couple has a happily ever after.

Of course, as I'd gotten older, I'd realized that those kinds of things didn't exist. Still, I'd hoped for a marriage like my parents at the very least. Theirs had been arranged, but I knew they cared for each other. I didn't know how deep that ran or what kind of love they had for each other, but I knew they had been faithful and I'd seen them share affection. If I could not marry the man of my choosing, at least I could take comfort in the fact that my parents had married the same way and had spent the last thirty years in a good marriage.

Not once had I considered the nightmare to come. Saja had a low crime rate and laws that quickly and harshly punished violent offenders. Domestic violence and child abuse were treated the same as any other violent crime. We had always prided ourselves on how safe our country was, for visitors as well as citizens. Even if I hadn't been a princess, I wouldn't have ever thought my future husband capable of hurting me. As princess, the idea had been ludicrous, unthinkable.

And yet, I'd had to carefully apply make-up on my arms and neck to cover the fading bruises. Even as I walked down the aisle towards Tanek, I experienced twinges of pain from his assault. It wasn't so bad that I let it show. Aside from not wanting anyone present to know how he'd hurt me, I refused to give Tanek the satisfaction of knowing I still felt it.

The thing was, I knew I wouldn't be able to avoid it later tonight. It was my wedding night, and consummation was expected. It didn't matter that he'd already fucked me, or that I hadn't been a virgin when he'd done it. We'd be expected to have sex, and there to be proof of it on our sheets tomorrow morning.

After the ceremony, there would be a reception where we would be expected to greet our guests and pretend to be content, if not happy. Even the regular people in Saja knew that the marriage was arranged, though I was sure most of them thought it was something romantic. The other high society people at the wedding would better understand the truth, but I would still be expected to play my part.

I pushed aside thoughts of what was to come and tried to focus on the now. I didn't exactly want to think about where I was now, but it was better than what was coming. I forced myself to focus on repeating the words my father said, a mix of the standard vows of several different religions. I didn't particularly care about any of them. I said what I had to say and that was enough.

When my father asked for anyone who protested the marriage to speak up, I tensed, half-expecting to hear Reed's voice declaring that I couldn't marry Tanek. I could imagine him saying he loved me and we were supposed to be together. I'd accepted my fate, but in that moment, I knew that if Reed had indeed shown up, I wouldn't have been able to turn him away.

I missed what my father said next, but I didn't need to hear it to know it had been him telling Tanek to kiss me. It was all I could do not to pull back and slap him as his mouth came down on mine. It was a fairly chaste kiss, the kind most would expect from a couple who barely knew each other, but it hadn't been our first. I hadn't been able to forget the feel of his lips, hard and demanding, his tongue nearly choking me.

I managed to get through the kiss without gagging and then took his arm as my father announced us. I allowed myself a quick moment to scan the crowd and my heart skipped a beat. Golden hair. Reed? Was it him, lurking in the shadows? Why would it be, though? I'd told him I'd made my choice. He'd probably been on a plane back to America that same afternoon. In fact, he was probably in bed with some gorgeous blonde right now, forgetting all about me.

Pain laced through me at the thought, but I kept a smile on my face. It wasn't a real one, but it was good enough to fool the people, if not my parents and my husband. Husband. I didn't even want to think the word, but I made myself dwell on it. I had no right to be jealous or hurt over anything Reed had done. I'd been the one who'd sent him away, who'd broken his heart.

Or maybe I was overestimating what we'd had, how he'd felt. Perhaps his heart had only been bruised alongside his ego. Perhaps I only wanted to think that he felt the same way I did, like my heart was being torn to shreds, every beat sending a new wave of pain through me. I'd felt like that from the moment I'd told Reed that I was choosing Tanek over him, and it had only gotten worse when Reed had showed up at the palace the next morning. Now, it was constant, a familiar presence that I'd almost become accustomed to. I wondered if I'd become numb to it after a while, and if that would be a blessing. Would not feeling anything be better than feeling what I felt?

Time began to move in jerky leaps and bounds as I found myself being moved from one table to another, shaking hands, kissing cheeks. The wealthiest and most influential of Saja's people were here. Some I knew well from seeing them at various functions over the years, others were strangers in all but name. It didn't matter though. They all wanted the same things: make sure the king and I both knew that they were present. The king for now, me for the future.

I danced and smiled, saying all the right things and behaving in a perfectly pleasant manner. I let Tanek put his hand on my arm and shoulders, pretending that I didn't find being near him repulsive. I smiled at my parents, pretending that I didn't hate them for what they were doing to me. I supposed I'd eventually forgive them, but at the moment, all I felt towards them was anger, and even that was not a strong enough word.

As evening turned into night, my father announced the end of the party. A few select guests were asked to stay, among them, my new in-laws. My already knotted stomach tightened even more. I knew what was coming next.

"We shall escort the new couple to the bridal suite," my father announced.

I allowed Tanek to take my arm and I curled my fingers under to keep anyone from seeing how badly my hands were shaking. My parents walked on either side of us, Tanek's parents slightly behind them. The others my parents had asked to stay were back there too, but I didn't look at them. The only positive thing I could feel was gratitude that Halea had been allowed to leave and not be a part of the processional.

When we reached the doors of what was to be our new room, Tomas and Kai were waiting. Bodyguards outside the bridal suite on the wedding night was another tradition, to ensure that no one interrupted the consummation. I had a suspicion that my parents had put them there as much to make sure I didn't run off. I wouldn't though. I still had Tanek's threat ringing in my ears. Even if I told them now what he had done, I didn't know that it would make a difference. They wouldn't believe me. Besides, my parents had already shown that they put the country above me. A divorce would tear things apart.

I lifted my chin. It didn't matter. It was done and I'd made my choice. This way, Halea would be safe and I would live with the consequences.

Tomas and Kai opened the double doors, bowing slightly as Tanek and I passed. As was tradition, the parents of the one marrying into the family walked over to the bed and, together, pulled down the covers. According to our history, it was done so that the parents could see that the sheets were pure white before the act. Tomorrow, they'd be removed from the bed and be packed away with all those nice bodily fluids that went along with consummation, kept as proof should there ever be a question of the marriage's legitimacy.

"May all higher powers, nature and the universe bless this union," my father said.

I really hated the way he tried to cover all his bases. I knew for a fact he was an atheist who liked to mock other religions in private, but to the country, he always tried to make it sound like he was open to everyone. That was his public face, the one I knew I'd have to put on someday. I didn't know what I believed, but I promised myself that whatever it ended up being, I wouldn't pretend otherwise. In one area of my life, at least, I'd be myself.

"May their union bring forth many children."

Tanek's mother gave the appropriate response to my father's statement.

I didn't look at Tanek as our families and the others turned and walked out. I waited until the doors closed before I took my arm from Tanek's. The room was lit with candles, giving me an eerie feeling of dejá vu. I remembered my dream. The way my heart had raced, my hands shaking. My pulse was beating fast now, and my hands trembled, but it wasn't the same. Before, it had been all about desire, passion, the need to join with him, to be complete. Now, it was fear and anger, each one warring for dominance.

Before either one could win, Tanek's hand was buried in my hair, pain shooting through my scalp. I let out a pained yelp and he twisted my neck around.

"Silence!" he hissed. "Your guards will remain outside the door all night and I do not think you would like what will happen if they interrupt."

I swallowed any other sound I might have made. I didn't know what exactly he would do, but I knew it wouldn't be good. Any hope I'd had that tonight wouldn't be painful for me had vanished, but at least Halea would be safe.

I clung to that thought as Tanek dragged me over to the bed. I couldn't completely suppress the pained moan when my knees struck the floor, but it wasn't loud enough to be heard. Cool air caressed my thighs as Tanek pushed my dress up around my waist.

"It is our wedding night," Tanek said as he yanked down my panties. "And I will have your virginity."

My mind didn't process his meaning until he spat and I felt his finger inside of me...not where I expected.

"I assumed you were not *that* much of a whore to your American men, and it seems I was right."

I grabbed the sheet and shoved it in my mouth just in time to stifle my scream.

Chapter 18

Reed

The white silk robe perfectly complemented her dusky skin, but she was even more beautiful without it than she was with it. I watched as the material slipped from her shoulders, revealing the body that had been haunting my every waking and sleeping moment.

"Why are you staring?" she asked as she sauntered towards me. "You have seen many women naked before, including me."

"Just enjoying knowing that you're mine."

One arm went around her waist, pulling her towards me. The other cupped the back of her head. Her mouth was soft and sweet under mine. She tasted of peaches and cream. Her breasts pressed against my chest, nipples already hard.

I slid my hand down to her ass, cupping the firm cheek. Her tongue curled around mine and I

pulled her more tightly against me. My skin burned
everywhere it touched hers and I walked her back
to our bed.

Our bed.

Our room.

I loved the word.

I loved her.

I kissed the top of her head and brushed a few
curls from her face. My family. Nami and our
children. They were all that mattered. I didn't care
if I lost everything else, as long as I had them...

I woke slowly, rolling towards the far side of the
bed, arm outstretched. For a few beautiful seconds, I
thought I could feel her next to me. My wife. And
our children would be waking soon, running in to
see if we were already up. Beautiful children with the
perfect blend of Nami and myself. Each one unique
and amazing. The family I'd always wanted.

My eyes opened as my fingers found the space
next to me cold and empty. With the sight came the
truth, hitting me hard enough that I struggled to
breathe. Nami was married, but not to me. She
would bear children, but not mine. The life I'd
imagined, the family in my dream, neither of them
were real. Pain shot through me, and I turned my
face towards my pillow. The future I'd thought I
would have had disappeared hours ago when Nami
had spoken her vows. All I had left now were

dreams, and the taste they left in my mouth was bitter.

For the first time, I wished I'd never met Nami Carr.

***

I considered staying in my hotel room and drinking alone, but knowing that Nami was probably, at this moment, preparing to go to bed with her new husband, I felt like drinking by myself would be an entirely new level of pitiful. I didn't feel like trying to find a club, mostly because it would remind me of how Nami and I had first met, but also because I didn't particularly want to be around people. I snorted a laugh. I was too proud to drink alone, but I didn't want anyone around either. A club was usually where people went to interact with others. I wanted to be left alone, which meant a bar.

I considered leaving the hotel and having a cab driver take me somewhere, but in the end, I didn't feel much like that either. Fortunately, the hotel had a bar and that was just a short walk from the elevators. I made my way down there after a shower and dressing. If I'd stayed in my room, I wouldn't have bothered with either.

I took a seat at the bar, as far from the television as possible. I didn't want to see all the news stories about this morning's festivities, or worse, speculation about what was occurring right now. I didn't want to think about what she was doing.

"Give me shot of the hard stuff and keep the bottle close by," I said to the bartender when he came my way. "The best you have."

He nodded and went for the top shelf stuff. I tossed back the first shot without even tasting it, but it burned on the way down and that was what I wanted. I went slower with the second, sipping at it and trying to savor the flavor. It was good, much better than I'd expected, and it wasn't anything I'd tasted before. When the bartender came back to fill my glass again, I asked him what I was drinking.

"Saja's finest rum," he said in thickly accented English. "We do not have much variety made here, but our quality is excellent."

"Yes, it is," I agreed. Judging by the pleasant buzz now going through my head, it was strong too, and at the moment, that's what I cared about.

I had a fairly high tolerance for alcohol. Not quite as much as some of my friends from back in college, but I could hold my own. People were often surprised at how much business was conducted with the assistance of alcohol, and the last thing anyone wanted to do was sign a contract while drunk.

Tonight, however, I didn't have any business to do, no reason to stay sober. I'd only been truly hammered a few times in my life, and none of them intentionally. Well, not until recently anyway. No matter why I'd done it, I hadn't particularly liked it, and I definitely hadn't liked the results the morning after, but I knew I was about to do it again. Despite knowing that I'd most likely spend all next morning hugging the toilet, I wanted the oblivion that only alcohol could offer.

I was a couple steps past tipsy and heading towards slurring and staggering when a tall, dark-haired woman sat down next to me. I blearily glanced at her out of reflex, but then turned back to my drink.

"American or European?"

Her voice was lower than I would've expected, husky in that sexy kind of way that I was sure made men sit up and take notice. Or at least had a similar effect on a specific body part.

I turned back towards her. It took my eyes a moment to focus and I knew I was pretty close to plastered. The alcohol didn't stop me, however, from appreciating a pretty face, or a killer body. She had to be at least five ten, but with curves rather than skinny. Her hair was black, not brown as I'd first thought, and long. Dark eyes and tanned skin. She was the sort of woman who men would fall over themselves for just a chance to get her in bed.

And apparently, my previous disinterest had intrigued her.

"American," I answered her question late, but

she hadn't taken her eyes off of me since asking it. "Reed."

"Lona." She held out her hand, palm down to let me know that she didn't want to shake.

I grasped her fingers and brushed my lips across the back of her hand. Good for me, I could still be smooth when I was drunk. She leaned towards me, giving me a good look at her ample cleavage. She was dressed sexy, but not slutty. I supposed there was still a possibility that she was a hooker working the hotel bar, but I was going to go with believing she found me attractive.

"Are you here on business?" She touched my knee. "Or pleasure?" Her fingers moved up my thigh.

I laughed and she gave me an amused look. "It wasn't business, but it definitely hasn't been a pleasurable trip either."

That wasn't entirely true, I knew. Images of Nami flashed into my head, memories of her beneath me, of her expression when she came. Until the moment she'd sent me away, the trip had been very much about pleasure.

"Perhaps I can change that," she said. Her hand curved around my thigh, her fingers brushing against my crotch.

I cocked my head and squinted at her, trying to figure out if she was hitting on me, or negotiating her rate for the night.

"I know what you are thinking." She slid her hand over and cupped my crotch. "And the answer is no."

"No?" I raised an eyebrow, spreading my legs open a bit more to allow her better access. Her fingers felt amazing.

"I am not asking for money." She stood and put her lips against my ear. Her breasts pressed against my arm.

"Then what is it you want?" I asked. She smelled like flowers and my nose twitched, wanting to sneeze.

"This." She squeezed my cock and teased my ear with her tongue.

"You just randomly come up to strangers in a hotel bar and grab their dicks?" The words came out a bit more directly than I'd intended, but then again, I hadn't really meant to say anything to begin with. I blamed the alcohol.

She grinned at me. "When my friends bet me that I cannot get the handsome American into bed, I do."

I returned the smile, wondering if it was as goofy as it felt. "I wouldn't want you to lose a bet on my account."

"I have a room," she said.

"You're a tourist?" I asked, surprised. I'd

thought her accent sounded like Nami's.

"Not precisely." She shook her head as she took my hand. "I am from the other side of Saja. My friends and I came for the wedding and did not want to drive home late."

My stomach lurched. "Wedding?"

"Ah, yes, you are not from here. The princess of Saja was married this morning."

"And you were invited?" Shit, that sounded rude. Still, I was more worried about keeping one foot steady in front of the other.

"I am a journalist," she said as we walked onto the elevator. "A small, online magazine, but all of Saja media was invited."

I grabbed her around the waist, spinning us so that her back was against the wall. The spinning wasn't good for my head, but the thought of having to listen to her talk about Nami's wedding was worse. I covered her mouth with mine, swallowing whatever else she was going to say.

She tasted like tequila. Her tongue danced with mine and she ground against my thigh, moaning at the friction. I moved down her neck, nipping at the skin there, biting and sucking until Lona's fake nails dug into my back hard enough to make me gasp.

The elevator doors dinged open and I pulled back. "This isn't my floor."

"No," she smiled. "It is mine."

Right. She'd mentioned a room. I let her lead me down the hallway, stealing a look down at her ass when she stopped in front of her door. Damn. She had all the right curves and an ass I could bounce a quarter off of.

For some reason, that idea struck me as funny and I barely suppressed a laugh. I didn't think Lona would be too happy if I started laughing like an idiot when I should've been concentrating on getting her out of her clothes.

When we stepped into the room, I quickly realized that wasn't going to be much of a problem. She apparently hadn't been expecting me to take off her clothes at all. She'd barely gone a few steps before she stripped off her dress and revealed that she hadn't been wearing anything underneath it.

Her skin was smooth and unblemished, her nipples a deeper shade of brown. She had the kind of body most men only dreamed of. And then she went down onto her knees.

"Fuck," I breathed.

"Yes," she said. "But I would like to taste you first."

Her hands made short work of my pants, tugging them down around my thighs and taking my underwear with them.

"Very nice," she said approvingly.

"You ain't seen nothing yet." If I'd been a bit

more sober, I would've thought the statement inane. Now, it just seemed witty.

She wrapped her hand around my cock. Even soft, I was bigger than average. She worked her hand over my shaft for a couple strokes, then leaned forward and took the head between her lips. I closed my eyes, trying to concentrate on the feeling of her mouth, the wet heat, the suction.

I couldn't just focus on the sensations though. It wasn't what I wanted. Lona knew what she was doing. Her hands and mouth did all the right things. But I didn't want someone who was skilled. I wanted passion, not just for my body, but for all of me. I wanted different hands, a different mouth. I could imagine Nami, the sight and feel of her, but my body didn't respond because I knew it was fake.

I sighed and opened my eyes. Lona was still lavishing attention on my cock, but I knew it wasn't going to work. I was half-hard, but that was purely physical. Between the alcohol I'd consumed and the thoughts of Nami, I wasn't going to be able to do this. I didn't want to do it.

I reached down and took Lona's arms, raising her to her feet. "I'm sorry," I said. I managed an embarrassed smile. "Too much to drink tonight."

I tugged myself back in, made a hasty exit from Lona's room and moments later I was heading back to the bar. I fully intended to continue drinking the rest of the evening. I would make sure by the end of the night I'd consumed enough alcohol so I wouldn't remember this mortifying day.

Chapter 19

Reed

I was a glutton for punishment. Stupidly masochistic. A moron bent on self-destruction. Basically, a fucking idiot.

For a reason that was still escaping me, I'd actually been in Saja for a week. A mother-fucking week. I should've left as soon as Nami told me she was choosing Tanek. But I'd stayed. Then I should've booked the first flight after I'd seen her go through with the wedding. But, no, I'd decided to stick around. Of course, any normal person with common sense would've grabbed any available seat to anywhere but here after the disastrous night I couldn't get it up.

As I'd already proven, however, I wasn't a normal person and I most certainly didn't have common sense. I used to. In fact, I had always considered myself to be the sensible one, the person who always made the right choices. Or, at least, I had been.

What had happened to that guy? I felt like every decision I've made lately had been the wrong one. When had I started fucking everything up? A part of me wanted to say that the bad choices had started here, or maybe in Europe, but I knew that I'd been making a mess of things before that. Had it been when I'd chosen Britni over Piper?

Or maybe I was lying to myself completely. Did I only think I was sensible before because I'd always made good business decisions? Because I'd always followed what my parents had told me to do? Was that why I kept fucking up my own decisions? Because I'd never learned how to make the right ones?

I squinted against the sun as I stepped outside the hotel. I squinted, pain spiking in my temples as I put on my sunglasses. I'd basically spent the entire past week hungover or drunk. I'd started Monday morning by buying some beer and heading down to the beach where I'd made my way through a six pack while checking out the gorgeous women who were sunbathing there. I'd eaten practically nothing, but had gotten another six pack for the rest of the day. I'd flirted with a couple women, but hadn't let it go any further than flirting. When the sun had begun to set, I'd headed back to my room, eating something from room service, then finished off whatever alcohol I'd had left.

Despite the way my head had pounded the next day, I'd decided that I'd liked what I'd done the day before. Things sort of blurred together after that. I would spend the day drinking and flirting on one of the most beautiful beaches I'd ever seen without caring about the view. I had people all around but, aside from the few women who'd come by to hit on me, no one talked to me. It was a great combination of being alone and being with people. I didn't have to worry about condemning looks while I drank, probably because everyone assumed I was on vacation. One of the things I'd learned while in Europe was that people didn't expect much of Americans in general, and even less of those on vacation.

I supposed I technically was on vacation. I wasn't working, after all. Could I really consider it a vacation since I'd quit with plans to start my own business? Or did the fact that I had absolutely no ambition at the moment and no concrete idea of what I wanted to do negate my original intentions?

I paid the clerk for my beer and tried to forget about the real world. I had plenty of money. Even staying here, it would take me years to burn through what I had. Unless, of course, I did something stupid. I'd known kids back in Philadelphia who'd blow thousands of dollars in a single night gambling or at a strip club. Then there were impulse buys like cars, but I wasn't in the mood to spend money on random things.

I found my usual spot on the beach taken and decided to head a bit further down. There was space here, but it was crowded enough that I didn't want to stay. Since it was a beautiful Saturday afternoon, I figured there'd be a lot of people on the beach, but it was even more crowded than I'd expected.

I sighed as I trudged through the sand, a beach towel under one arm, my beer under the other. The sun was overhead and I could feel the rays beating down on me. Sweat glistened on my skin as I made my way around scantily-clad men and women sunbathing, kids playing catch and a few families eating lunch. The sandy beach was starting to turn into an area that was a bit more rocky, and therefore less desirable, but there were still people setting up.

I crossed over to a large boulder that sat against a gradually rising cliff and decided this was far enough. I didn't care about getting to the water, so the rocks between me and the ocean weren't a problem, and the breeze that blew in was strong and cool.

I spread the towel at the base of the boulder and sat down, leaning back against the cool rock. The cliff offered only a small bit of shade, but it was enough. I cracked open a beer and settled in to people watch. Or, more accurately, stare at the ocean and pretend that I cared about life in general. Little thoughts would sometimes creep in, whispers asking what I was going to do next, reminding me that I couldn't exactly stay in Saja indefinitely. I was a tourist, not a citizen, and I'd eventually have to leave. Whenever any of those thoughts occurred, I'd take another drink.

I had a bit of a buzz going on by mid-afternoon, but I was still sober. Sober enough to be interested when I heard a murmur going through the crowd. I stood up and began walking towards the noise. I didn't know what was going on, but it sounded like it would be a good distraction and that's what I really needed.

I was at the back of the crowd, trying to see over a throng of heads, when I heard someone say a word I recognized even though it wasn't in English.

"...Namisa..."

My stomach flipped and I suddenly wished I'd eaten something this morning. The beer I'd drank was sloshing around, threatening to make a reappearance. It couldn't be true, I told myself. Nami was on her honeymoon. Someone must've just been talking about the wedding and it had nothing to do with the commotion I was hearing. Even if she was back from her honeymoon, she wouldn't be here, on a beach. She'd be off with her new husband doing wife things or queen preparation or whatever the hell it was someone like her did.

Then the crowd parted and I saw her.

Bodyguards surrounded her, moving people out of the way both by their presence as well as physically when some didn't move fast enough. I didn't see Tomas or Kai, but I supposed they were probably enjoying their time at home since they'd been gone for so long. If anyone deserved a vacation, it was those two. I wasn't particularly fond of either of them, but they'd spent years with Nami, almost constantly on duty. It couldn't have been easy.

The new guards – or at least new for me – weren't as big as Tomas and Kai, but they weren't exactly little either. Still, I could see Nami in the center.

I could tell something wasn't quite right just by the way she was walking. Shoulders hunched forward, arms around her waist. Her head was down, eyes on the ground. As she drew closer, I could see other physical differences. She was wearing a classically cut dress, a bit too fancy for the beach, I would've thought, but definitely something appropriate for a princess when she was out and about with her subjects. I knew it had to have been made specifically for her, but I could see now that it didn't fit right, as if she'd lost weight since she'd last worn it. The color should've been perfect for her too, but her skin was pale, as if she'd been ill.

I felt a flash of concern. Was she sick? It would explain everything, but I couldn't figure out why she'd be walking on the beach if she was ill. Surely the royal family had private physicians who would've made sure she stay in bed until she recuperated fully. And even if he or she had recommended exercise, I doubted this would've been the place to go. The palace had beautiful grounds she could've walked around.

She was almost directly across from me and I could see the bags under her eyes. She hadn't been sleeping well. A pain went through me. Of course she hadn't. She'd been married for a week. She and her husband had probably been busy trying to get that all-important heir to the throne. The thought of it made me want to throw up.

I started to turn away, not wanting to risk her seeing me. The last thing I needed was for her to realize I'd stuck around like some love-sick loser. As I started to go, however, I saw something else out of the corner of my eye. No one else would've caught it because no one knew her body like I did. I'd memorized it, dreamed of it.

On her upper arm, not quite covered by her sleeve, was a bruise. She'd used make-up on it, but I could still see it. As she shifted, her sleeve moved and I could clearly identify the shape.

Fingers.

Rage filled me, driving away everything else I'd been feeling. It all made sense now. Her appearance, the way she held herself. Why she'd seemed distant, different. The bastard was hurting her, and there was nothing I could do to stop him. Or was there?

The End of Vol. 2

Don't miss the final installment, Exotic Desires Vol. 3, release June 2nd.

Other book series from M. S. Parker

Casual Encounter Box Set
Sinful Desires Box Set
Club Prive Vol. 1 to 5
French Connection (Club Prive) Vol. 1 to 3
Chasing Perfection Vol. 1 to 4
Broken Pleasures
Forbidden Pleasures
His Pleasures
Dark Pleasures
More Pleasures – release April 24th
Pure Pleasures – release May 12th
Exotic Desires series – release April/May 2015

Acknowledgement

First, I would like to thank all of my readers. Without you, my books would not exist. I truly appreciate each and every one of you.

A big "thanks" goes out to all my Facebook fans, street team, beta readers, and advanced reviewers. You are a HUGE part of the success of my series.

I have to thank my PA, Shannon Hunt. Without you my life would be a complete and utter mess. Also a big thank you goes out to my editor Lynette and my wonderful cover designer, Sinisa. You make my ideas and writing look so good.

About The Author

M. S. Parker is a USA Today Bestselling author and the author of the Erotic Romance series, Club Privè and Chasing Perfection.

Living in Southern California, she enjoys sitting by the pool with her laptop writing on her next spicy romance.

Growing up all she wanted to be was a dancer, actor or author. So far only the latter has come true but M. S. Parker hasn't retired her dancing shoes just yet. She is still waiting for the call for her to appear on Dancing With The Stars.

When M. S. isn't writing, she can usually be found reading– oops, scratch that! She is always writing. ☺

Printed in Great Britain
by Amazon

30191201R00108